True

PLAYER

For Real

Publishing

Theastarr Valerie

ISBN: 979-8-9853583-2-2

Edited by Akilah Valerie

Cover design by Empress Royále Publishing

Empress Royále Publishing
empressroyalepublishing@gmail.com
facebook.com/empressroyalepublishing
instagram.com/empressroyalepublishing

"Everything tells a story; let us help you tell your story to the world."

First Day To Do List:
Jet Black
Brunette
Party
KH
Conquest
Anatomy

There is something about a woman that excites me. I can't just have one...

~ **The Hunter**

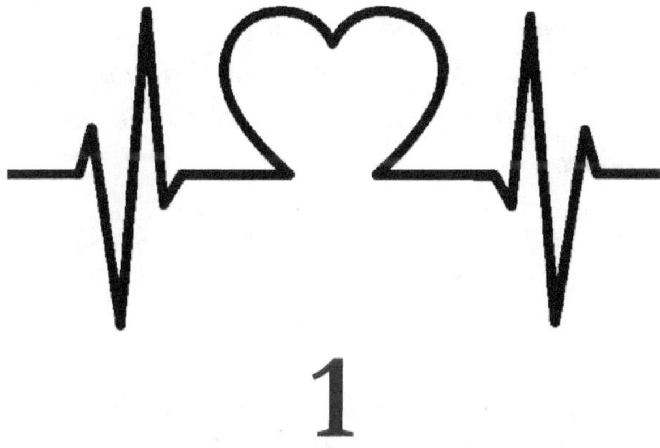

1

Freshman Year
Semester One

College is a player's paradise...

Kage enters the university building winking at every girl in sight. Girls from all over the world would be attending this campus. For now, he opted to stick with the ones from Starr Islands. He grinned at the endless possibilities…

"Welcome to GSIU. My name is Xerses. I will be your campus tour guide. It is tradition for the upperclassmen to conduct these orientations. Who knows, maybe one day you could be standing here."

Jet black. Red. Blonde. Brunettes. Hmmmm. All my types. Oh. I'm supposed to be paying attention to what he is saying.

"Sup man. Do you have any questions?" Xerses asks. "Are you a citizen of Grand Sierra Isla?"

"Yo, slow down son. I don't even care about all this. I'm ready to PARTY! This place is crawling with shorties—"

"That's not what college is about. What's your name?"

"Kage Hunter," he says, popping his collar. "I'm a *true player for real.*"

"I hear you," Xerses scoffs. "What's your major?"

"Anesthesiology."

"That's cool. Never met any freshman with that major."

Kage rolls his eyes. "Do you usually talk this much? I just wanna unpack and check out the club scene."

"Let me see your room and board card." Xerses scans it. "Well look at that… we're going to be roommates."

Why am I not surprised? I get placed in a room with the most annoying nerd on planet earth.

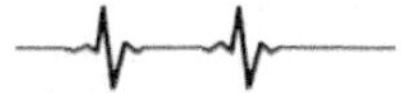

"This is Casa Di Xerses."

"You named your room?" Kage laughs. "Man, you need a life."

"I have one. Your freshman orientation starts in 20 minutes. Grab a bite and don't be late."

Seriously. Who is this dude?

"Xerses," a female calls out, "are you going to meet us downstairs for lunch?"

"Just a minute, Nouvel."

Kage jumps off the bed and peeks out the door.

Yoooo, who is THAT natural beauty?

Xerses comes back in. "Aight, later man."

"Wait, wait, wait, wait… Friend. Buddy. Who was that exotic goddess that just hollered at you?"

"That's my baby sister. OFF LIMITS! Don't even THINK about it. I will literally kill you. There are other girls on campus, do whatever you want, but let my sister be invisible to you. GOT IT?"

"I can't make any promises. That's my future wife," he laughs.

He grabs Kage's collar. "I'm serious. I will **KILL** you."

"Whatever, dude," Kage shrugs.

That chick right there is NUMBER ONE on my conquest radar. How is it that such a beauty would have a brother that looks like him?

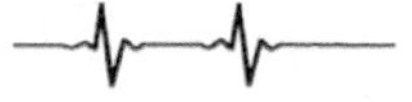

"Freshman Orientation 101 is designed to teach you the ins and outs of university. You will work with a TA who will give you insight on what it takes to make it through your four years here…" the professor announces.

Finally. He's done talking…

"Hi, my name is Ember. What's yours?"

"You can call me **whatever** you want," Kage flirts. "I'm loving the red and blonde highlights. Edgy!"

"Awkward. Look ***little*** boy. I'm a SOPHMORE, you're a baby. Know your place."

"Age is just a number."

Ember rolls her eyes. "I'm in no mood for this."

Kage watches her exit the auditorium. "Hmmm, mmm, mmm, look at the body on her."

By the time this stupid class is over I'd have already checked her off my list. Mark my words.

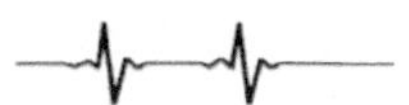

Xerses spots Kage in the hallway. "How was the orientation?"

"I met a TA and she's definitely on the ***Hunter's radar***. She had the nerve to tell me that she's too old for me."

"The girls on this campus are different. Special bred. They come to school already betrothed."

"I don't care. That's not going to stop me. What about your sister? Is she one of those ***special*** girls?"

"We don't come from this country so her upbringing was different. However, Nouvel's standards are high. You're not even a **possible** contender to even stand on the line of men interested in her."

"One day you'll eat your words. I WILL get her."

Xerses laughs. "That'll take a miracle. One I'm afraid is not going to happen."

"We'll see. It's her decision, not yours."

"Trust me, Kage, my sister will never be with a guy like you. Set your sights on someone with low standards…"

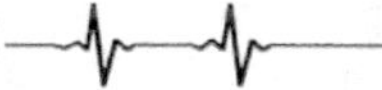

"Ember, how was the orientation?" Nouvel inquires.

"Meh. It was going okay until I met a stupid freshman boy who still has milk on his face, trying to chat me up. I all but laughed at his pathetic attempts."

"You always have some guy chatting you up. That must feel great. No one even looks my way."

"Why you lying, Nouvel?"

They both laugh.

"Does that sound convincing? I have to ace this audition."

"You'll get it. You're dramatic beyond words."

"Thank you. Thank you…" Nouvel bows. "I'm heading out now."

"Good luck," Ember replies.

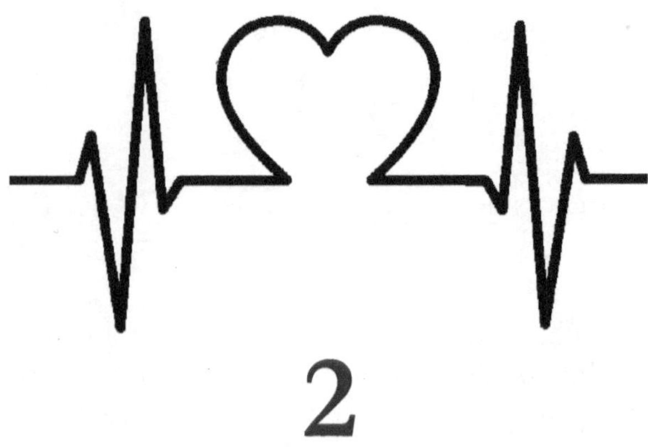

2

Promenade

Kage sees Nouvel walking to the Theatre Building. He paces himself to walk with her. "Sup sweetness."

"Um, hi."

He wipes a hand on his pants, then stretches it out to shake hers. "My name is Kage Hunter, what's yours?"

"Nouvel de Amico. I'm sorry I was on my way to an audition. Can't stop for small talk."

"OUCH! Small talk?"

Nouvel walks away and leaves him speechless.

If this chick thinks she can ignore KAGE, she's mistaken.

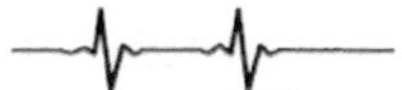

Inside the building, Kage spots Nouvel and sits next to her. "Why you acting like that?"

"Like what exactly? Look here, ***Kage Hunter***, I can sense your type the moment you stepped off the plane and landed on this soil. PLEASE don't waste my time."

"You high maintenance chicks think cuz you all beautiful you can speak to men however you want. Babygirl, I can get ANY woman I want. You're not important."

Nouvel claps sarcastically. "WOW. Are you a drama major? I felt the passion in your voice; almost convincing… I don't care about what woman you can get. I'm not your *babygirl* so please have some respect. Grow up. This is university. Only boys are players. Goodbye!"

Can't be wasting my time with girls like Nouvel. That's a headache in itself…

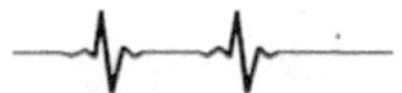

"Gym's closed."

Kage turns to see a girl in navy shorts and a sports bra. His eyes widen.

"Sorry," he shrugs. "First time here. I didn't pay attention to the clock. What's your name?"

"You really have to go," she replies, trying not to look at his bulging pecs.

"Like what you see?" he winks.

The girl begins to fiddle with her phone.

"What time do you get off?" Kage continues.

"Please leave."

Kage walks up to her ear. "Let's go to my place."

"I can't."

"I'll make it worth your while."

"Please… I can't," she exhales.

He winks at her.

"Okay," she smiles. "Give me a few minutes to lock up."

That was too easy. Betrothed… HA! What a joke…

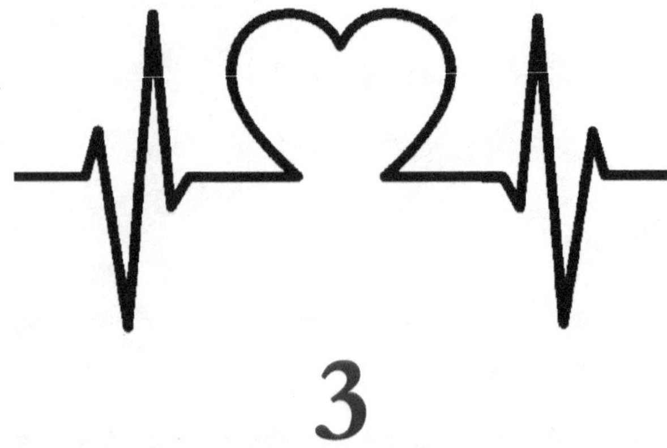

3

Casa Di Xerses

"You have to get outta here," Kage barks.

"Why?" the girl from the gym, answers.

"If my roommate sees you, there's gonna be some problems."

"When am I going to see you again?"

"You know this was a one-time thing," Kage scoffs. "I said *no strings attached—*"

Xerses opens the door. "Are you kidding?"

"I told her to leave," Kage counters.

"Kage, I don't care how you live your life, but you're making me look bad. I have a reputation. I said NO GUESTS! What don't you understand?" Xerses snaps.

"Sorry man... You gotta go!" Kage says to the girl.

"Are you gonna call me?"

Kage replies with silence.

"Do you even know my name?" she asks.

He shrugs. "Save yourself the embarrassment and just leave."

"Bayou, my name is Bayou."

"Babygirl, your name matters not," Kage chuckles. "GO!"

The girl hurriedly puts on her clothes. "You're a STUPID JERK YOU KNOW THAT, KAGE HUNTER. I hope you—"

Kage laughs out loud, as he pushes her out the door.

Xerses wrinkles his nose. Opening the fridge, he takes a swig of *Lemon Blitz*. "Girls like that will never make good wife material. They come with too much baggage."

"I ain't judging."

"Of course not, you have no standards."

"When was the last time you got some?"

"Been there, done that. Now my focus is on graduating."

"Hold up," Kage gestures, "Mr. Perfect Xerses was a player?"

"Don't let that perverted mind of yours turn. I was in a long-term relationship—"

"BORING!" Kage fake snores.

Xerses rolls his eyes.

"I'm sorry man, continue."

"She cheated."

"And that stopped you from pursuing others? You're an **upperclassman**," he mocks. "I'm sure you have girls lining up to be with you."

"Therein lies the problem. I'll be graduating this year and I need to find someone to build a legacy with."

"Legacy smegacy. Did you grow up in a nerd convention or something? What about your sister?"

Xerses shoots him a look. "Don't ask about her."

"Come on man, a sexy chick like that must have men in and out of her room." He observes Xerses balling up his fists. "Sorry man. I'm just saying… you can't possibly think she's a virgin—"

"SHE IS!"

"How could you be so sure?" Kage counters.

"I know my sister, how we were raised, and her standards. Besides, she has a boyfriend who I'm 100% sure she's going to marry."

Kage laughs. "You don't know do you?"

"This conversation is over."

"I know every older brother **wants** their little sister to remain *innocent*, but the truth is you have no control over that."

"I SAID ENOUGH!"

"Aight, aight, I'm done."

"No more guests…"

"Whatever man," Kage retorts.

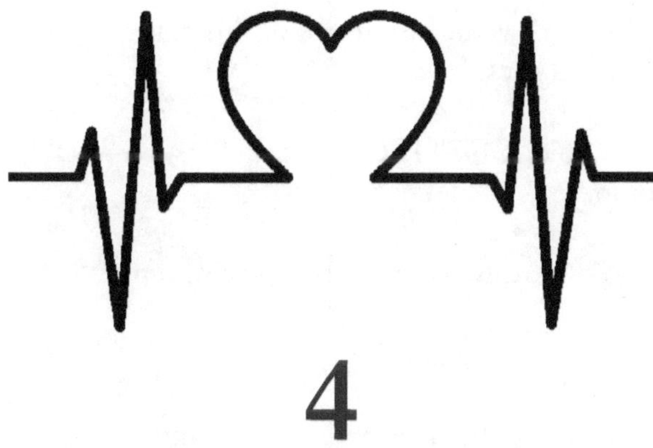

4

Nouvel stares at her phone.

“Still nothing?” Ember asks.

“I don’t get it. Rayce and I have been dating for over a year and this is the first time he’s ignored my calls.”

“Girl chill, maybe he has exams or something.”

“It’s the first week of school. We don’t have exams.”

“Why don’t you go to his dorm and see if he’s there?”

"I don't want him to think I'm being clingy," Nouvel says.

"You'd BETTER go check up on YOUR man."

"You know what Ember, you're right."

"Of course I am," she laughs.

Nouvel grabs her cell phone and exits the room.

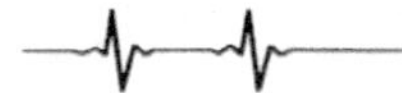

"Babes, are you there?"

No answer.

"Please tell me he isn't cheating. If I catch him cheating…"

"Nouvel? What are you doing here?"

"I tried calling, but you didn't pick up so I came to see—"

"If I was cheating, huh?"

"W-what?" Nouvel stutters. "Why would you think that?"

"I know you. Anytime you don't get what you want you jump to the worst conclusions," he says, kissing her forehead.

"Why didn't you answer your phone?"

"It was dead and I left it to charge. Ran out to get some groceries for our picnic later. Don't tell me you forgot."

"Uh haha," Nouvel counters. "Sorry babes. I'm trying to get the main role for the campus web series. With that in my portfolio, I will be set come senior year."

"I know you work hard. My girl's going to be a star. Maybe you'll end up starring in a big movie in *Vias*."

"Don't joke around. You know that's my goal. A lot's riding on this. My parents already think I'm throwing my life away by becoming an actress."

"What did they have in mind?"

"If I could be a NUN, they'd be happy. Being a *de Amico* is pressure. I gotta live up to Saint Xerses."

"Hey, cut my boy some slack."

"Whatever, are we going on the picnic now?"

"Later," he says, smacking her butt.

"Hands off, mister! You know that's for marriage."

"It looks so good though."

Nouvel laughs. "I can't help it if I'm cute," she says, doing a little dance.

"Promise never to cheat on me."

"You're the only one for me." Nouvel kisses him.

"That's not a promise."

"I...promise..."

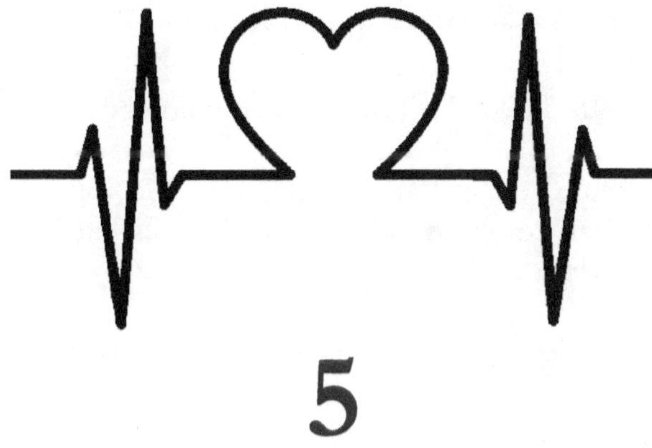

5

Four Weeks Later

"Don't tell anyone that we're messing around," Ember says, buttoning her shirt.

"Why would I do such a thing?" Kage grins.

"I can't believe I'm seeing a freshman."

"You're a sophomore, barely that much older. Besides, I'm *mature* for my age," he chuckles.

"Whatever. Just don't tell anyone about us, okay? It's against campus policy. I could get in a lot of trouble."

"Freshman Orientation is over."

"But, I'm still a TA," Ember counters.

"Fine," Kage says, kissing her. "So long as we can continue these late-night calls, my lips are sealed."

"At least you didn't take me to a cheap motel."

"I'm a Hunter. Just because I'm a freshman, you think I'm poor?"

"Where'd you get money to afford such a lavish hotel stay?"

"Don't worry about that… And no, I'm not doing anything illegal."

"Great." She touches his face. "Cuz I know that pretty mug of yours won't last one minute in jail."

They laugh.

"Time for you to go. My next call is on her way."

"I thought I was your *one and only*?"

"Yeah," Kage nods. "For *this* **moment**. But I have a list… Now go…"

"Same time next week?" Ember asks.

"Same time next week," he winks.

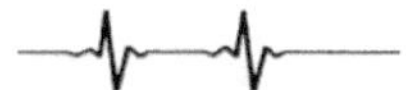

"Where were you? It's 4AM."

"Are you my mother?" Ember snaps.

"Sorry for caring."

"No you're not. You just want to rub it in my face that you have a boyfriend and I don't."

"Are you drunk?" Nouvel scoffs.

"Do I smell drunk to you?"

"You don't want to know how you smell."

"Oh wow," Ember claps. "Tell me how you really feel."

"What has gotten into you?"

"If you must know, I've been seeing a guy on and off for the past few weeks."

"Anyone I know?" Nouvel asks.

"Just some guy from campus."

"Why can't you tell me his name?"

"You're too judgmental."

"ME? Judgemental? I'm the **last** person to judge anyone."

Ember laughs, "Oh please, little miss perfect. What wrong have you done? You and your brother are known saints on this campus."

"Is that what people think of us?"

"Yes, *Saints de Amicos.* That's your nickname."

"Wow, and here I thought my best friend would have my back."

"Can I go to sleep now?"

"Whatever."

Ember holds her head as she walks to the room.

"Saint de Amico?" Nouvel whispers.

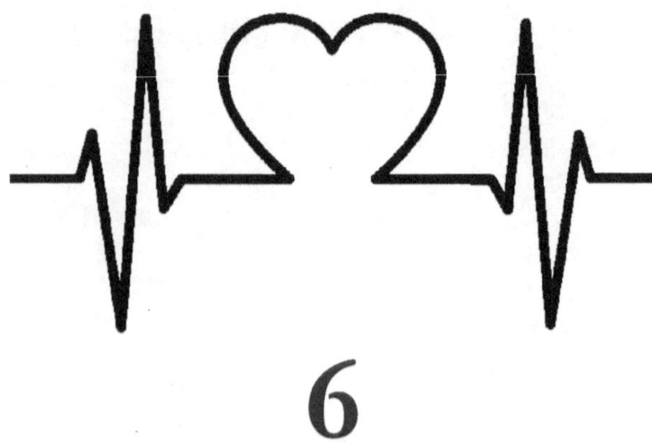

6

"Mr. Hunter, congratulations. You received the highest marks on the exam."

"Thank you, professor."

"That was a hard exam. No one's ever gotten 100% on their first try in all my years of teaching."

"Sorry to disappoint you."

"No, no. I was wondering if you'd like to head a study group for some of the other students. Sometimes we learn better from our peers."

"What's in it for me?"

"The satisfaction of helping others… Experience?"

"Nah, I'll pass. Besides, tutoring will mess up my extra-curricular activities."

"What are they?" he asks. "Maybe I can ask your professors to make accommodations for you."

"That won't be necessary. Sorry, I gotta go."

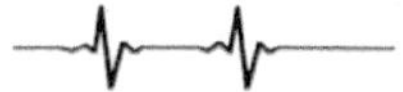

"I thought he'd never let you leave…"

"Huh?" Kage turns around to see a shapely ginger. "HELLO sweetness, what's your name?"

"Names are futile. Is it true what you told the professor?"

"About?"

"Not having time to tutor?"

"Interested? Kage flirts.

She nods. "I need to past the next exam or I could lose my scholarship."

"Gimme your number and I'll see what I can do."

"Thank you Kage," she says, planting a seductive kiss on his cheek.

"Wow, all of that for a tutor?"

"No, that's for my future boyfriend."

"Who? Me?"

She smiles.

"Babygirl, I don't do monogamy."

"That's okay, I don't mind sharing… *for a bit.*"

Kage rubs his hands together. A grin plastering his face. "Shall we?" he says, draping his arm around her waist.

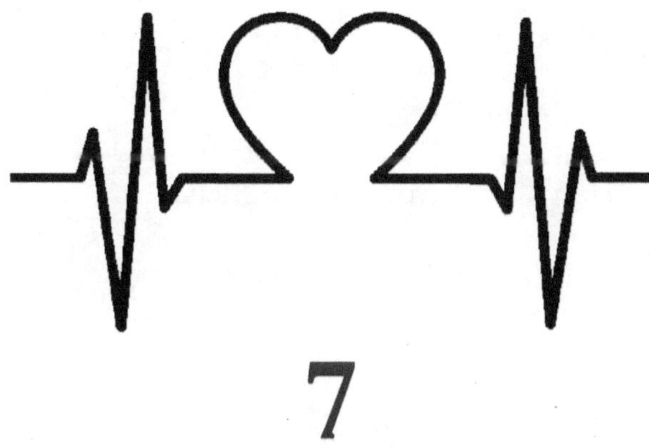

7

"What do you mean you can't see me?" Ember snaps.

"I sort of have a girlfriend."

"EXCUSE ME? No Kage, we have an arrangement."

"Sorry, I said no attachments. You've broken that. You used to be fun, now you're all clingy."

"Does she know you've been **sexing** half the campus?"

"Will you keep your voice down?" Kage demands. "Babygirl, the room's all yours."

"I don't want to stay in this room alone."

Kage shrugs.

"How DARE you get a girlfriend."

"What's wrong with me *settling down*?"

"You're 18, what do you know about exclusivity?"

"Hey, she knows how to ***put it down***," he gestures.

"You've already had sex with her?"

"Obviously. Or my name isn't Kage Hunter."

"You're really saying **NO** to me?" Ember counters.

"I'm just saying that our arrangement is off...***for now***. I don't know how long it'll last with her."

"Kage, DON'T DO THIS!" Ember yells.

"Why you trippin'?"

"NO! We had an arrangement. Please Kage," Ember says, grabbing his neck, to kiss him.

"You're embarrassing yourself. Let go of me."

"NO KAGE!"

"Ember, STOP! I don't want to hurt you."

In a rage, she punches him. "You will **REGRET** saying no to me. MARK MY WORDS!"

Kage grimaces. ***Stupid girl...***

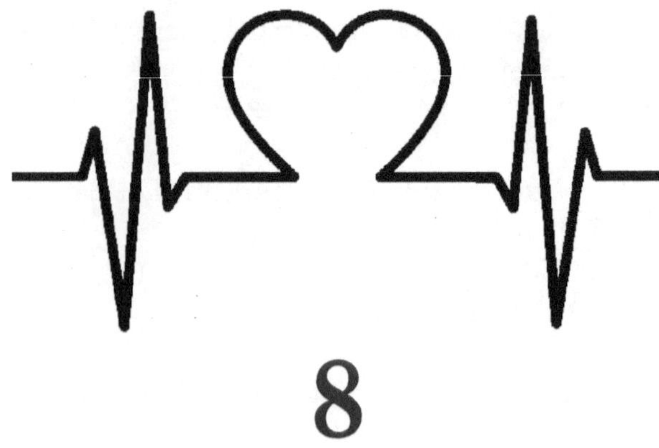

8

Nouvel observes her bestie sulking on the couch. "What's wrong?"

Ember shrugs.

"Talk to me," she says, sitting next to her.

"You don't care," Ember sobs.

"Yes, I do. Why are you crying?"

"Remember that guy I was telling you about?"

Nouvel nods.

"He just broke up with me."

"Oh honey, I'm sorry. Did he tell you why?"

"He said he has a ***girlfriend***."

Nouvel looks at her sympathetically. "Was he cheating on her?"

"I wish. He said they just got together. I'm trying to figure out who it could be. Literally dying inside."

"It can't be that bad. I've never seen you act this way before."

"He did something to me, girl." She blows her nose in a tissue.

"I'm so sorry. You seem to really like him."

"More like **love**."

"Ember, *in love?* You're joking right?"

"No. What we have is special. All of our times together have been magical."

"Come on girl, you gotta tell me who he is. Ain't no guy on campus that good."

"He is DEAD to me," Ember barks.

"Well, if you want to talk, I'm here."

"Oh please," Ember scoffs. "You just want to rub it in my face how great Rayce is."

Nouvel tilts her head. "What does he have to do with this?"

"You think you're better than me because you actually have a rich boyfriend."

"I don't care about his wealth, you know that."

"Yeah right."

"I'm serious," Nouvel counters.

"I could've been with Rayce, you know."

"So, you want my man now? Is that what you're telling me?"

"Don't nobody want him. I'm just saying that I had a chance to be his girlfriend."

Nouvel walks to the door. "Okay, forget all of that. We're going out."

"Let me sulk," Ember whines.

"Nah, let's go out and have some fun."

Ember wipes her eyes. "Please leave me…"
"Nope, we're going out." Nouvel grabs Ember's hand.

CLUB ILLUSION
PRESENTS
LADIES NIGHT
FRIDAY | 10 PM
TICKETS $20 | LADIES FREE

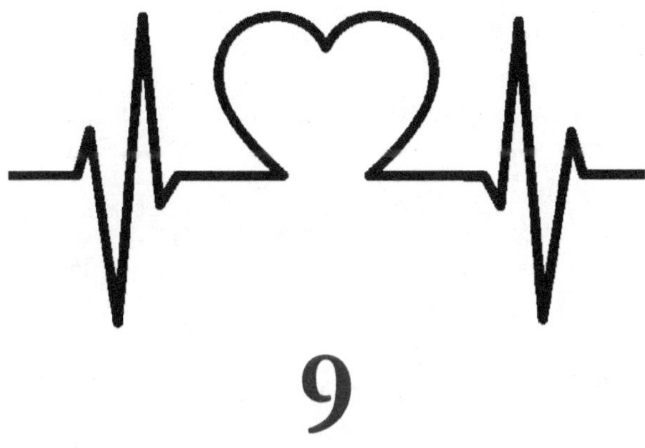

9

The music pulsated as Kage pushed through the clubgoers with Meadowlynn, his girlfriend of a few weeks. Of course, he never expected to be "tied down" with one girl. But she definitely knew how to keep him happy. So, he had no complaints.

"I'm going to get us some drinks," Kage says, kissing her cheek.

"Okay honey, I'll go freshen up."

"No need to."

"Stop it," Meadowlynn blushes.

"Hurry back. All these girls look thirsty for a dance with me. I feel vulnerable," he laughs.

"You're so full of it, Mr. Hunter."

"I love it when you call me mister," Kage winks.

Meadowlynn kisses him passionately.

"What was that for?"

"To let the ladies know that you're **mine**!"

"I'm sure they got the memo…"

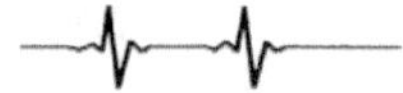

"Oh no, it's him," Ember gasps.

"Who?" Nouvel says, turning around. The club was jam packed. She didn't notice anyone in particular.

"The guy who dumped me."

"Let me at him."

Ember points.

Nouvel follows her finger. "You've gotta be kidding. Your guy is the ***freshman***?" She bursts out laughing. "That's a new low, even for you."

"Whatever. Laugh all you want. Everyone can't have a ***Rayce*** in their life. We take what we can get."

"Girl don't give me that. You could have any man on campus."

"It's different with Kage."

"I honestly don't wanna know," Nouvel mocks.

"I'm going to talk to him."

"Don't embarrass yourself."

Ember slaps Nouvel's hand. "Get off of me."

"Fine, if you want to be humiliated, then go right ahead."

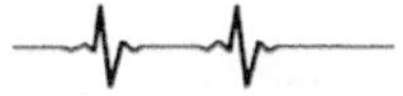

"What do you want, Ember?" Kage asks.

"Let's dance," she says, rubbing her body on him.

He pushes her away. "We're done. I'm here with my girl."

"You're gonna do me like that?"

"Baby, is this girl bothering you?" Meadowlynn asks, when she returns.

"She's no one."

Meadowlynn wrinkles her nose. "Be gone sweetie, Kage doesn't want you."

Ember exhales profusely, glaring at Kage, "You embarrassed me one too many times."

"Whatever… Meadowlynn, are you ready to dance?"

Ember grits her teeth as she watches them dance. "He's going to be very sorry…"

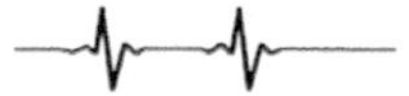

"What happened?"

"Let's go, Nouvel. I can't stay here."

"We just got here."

"Come on," Ember mumbles.

"Can I at least get my purse?" she scoffs.

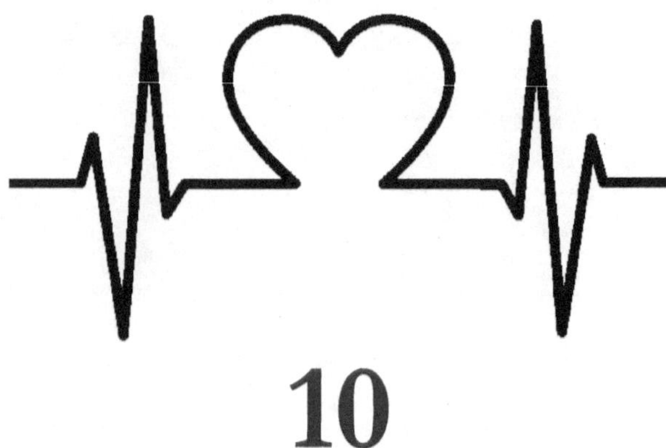

10

Meadowlynn strokes Kage's face as he laid in her lap.

He jumps up. "I have a great idea. Let's go away for the weekend."

"Baby, what are you talking about? I have exams coming up."

"I hardly get to spend time with you. You're always studying."

"Um, we ***are*** in university."

"We can study over the weekend. My family has a beach house on the coast."

"What exactly does your parents do? You seem to be really wealthy for a freshman."

"I'll tell you about it, once as you come with me."

Meadowlynn touches her chin. "Let me think about it."

"No thinking," he says, kissing her hand. "I want to spend time with you. Can't exactly bring you in ***Casa Di Xerses***. And our time here is short because of your roommate."

"Why do you live on campus? I mean you could afford to stay wherever you want."

"I am here on a scholarship. Why would I pay for a place, when I can stay here for free? I'm no idiot. My money has to last a long time."

"My baby is ***fione*** and good with money. How did I get so lucky?"

Kage kisses her. "I'm the lucky one."

"I'll go, BUT ***no funny business***."

"Oh, come on," Kage protests.

"Nope. A weekend of studying," she giggles.
"We'll see about that…"

"Yes, we will, Mr. Hunter. Yes, we will."

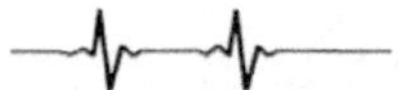

"Where are you heading?" Xerses inquires.

"Going out with my lady for the weekend."

"You really seem to like Meadowlynn."

"Why do you care so much about my love life?"

"Well, since you've been dating her, you haven't brought anyone into our dorm. I can breathe easy knowing that there's no sexual toxicity in my home."

"You ***really need*** to get some," Kage chuckles.

"Sex isn't all there is to life."

"I'm sorry, WHAT?"

"You heard me. One day you're going to look back and regret that list you have."

Kage laughs, looks at Xerses, then laughs again. "Wow, you're serious. What man regrets having sex?"

"I hope one day you grow up. You're a smart guy."

"Hey," Kage shrugs, "smart guys have sex too."

"Whatever man, I'm leaving. Don't forget to lock up."

"Yes, dad," Kage grins.

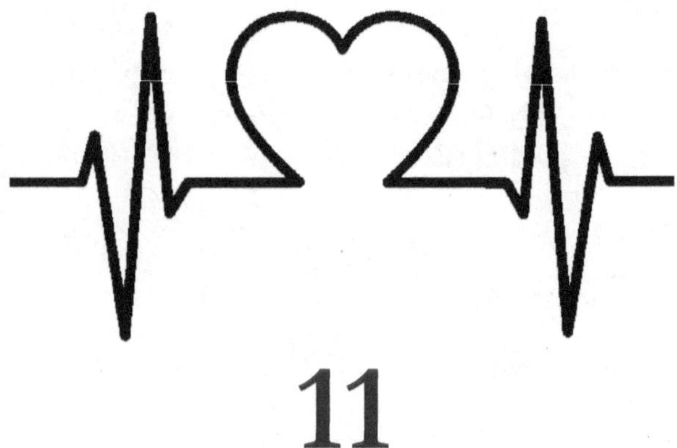

11

Later That Night

"Hey Ember, is Nouvel home?" Xerses asks. "I tried calling her cell, but she didn't pick up."

"I think she's out with Rayce."

"Is it okay if I wait here?"

"Sure, come in. Want something to drink?"

"*Grape Blitz* is okay," he says, closing the door.

"Sorry, we only have lemon."

"That's fine, I'll take whatever you have."

She hands him the can. "Have you seen Kage?"

"Why do you ask?" He looks at her. "I hope you're not falling for him."

"No, I'm a TA, remember."

"Yeah, but orientation finished a long time ago."

"I'm still a TA, and his professor asked that I speak to him about an assignment he missed," she lies.

"Well, I don't know much about his study habits. He never seems upset about his grades so I thought he was on top of things."

"Is he at home? I can stop by."

"You'll be wasting your time. Kage went out of town with his girlfriend."

"WHAT?! He's still seeing her?"

"Are you okay?"

"Sorry, I'm just upset that he's not focusing on his schoolwork."

"Wow, you take your position as a TA very seriously."

"I do," she nods. Ember grabs her jacket.

"Where are you off to?"

"I just remembered; I have a meeting."

"At 10PM?"

"Hey, I'm not in charge of meeting hours. You can stay here and wait for Nouvel if you want."

"Maybe I'll come back in the morning. I'm tired anyway. I don't think it's appropriate for me to be in any woman's place at this time."

"Woman? Nouvel is your sister."

"I'm talking about you."

"Whatever, I don't have time to argue with *Saint Xerses...*"

She closes the door behind them. They walk down the hallway.

"Saint?"

Ember nods. "You're *too perfect.* People ask questions."

"Like what?" He stops in front of her.

"I have somewhere to be."

"What kind of questions?"

"Does Xerses like girls?"

"Wow, my sexuality is questioned because I'm not promiscuous?"

"Duh! We are in university. This is prime exploration time."

"I've already experienced that lifestyle and got burned in the process," Xerses informs.

"She wasn't right for you."

"STI's are real. I don't want to live my life wearing *protection* because I can't keep it in my pants. Sex can wait. Right now, I'm focused on graduating and building my legacy. The last thing I need is for a bunch of girls to have me as part of their 'past loves'. No woman is going to ruin my future with **any** type of accusations."

"OKAY. OKAY. I hear you. You're definitely *one of a kind,* Xerses."

"And I like it that way. They can watch, but not touch. If more men did that, the world would be a better place."

"Tell your roommate that," she scoffs.

"What?"

"Don't worry about it." Her car beeps. "Later."

He waves as she drives off.

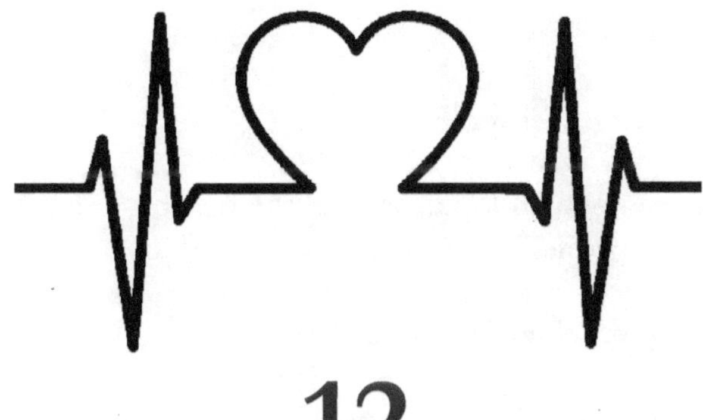

12

Kage and Meadowlynn hold hands as they walk down the beach.

"I'm glad that you suggested that we go away."

"I told you so," he smiles.

"What time is it?" she yawns.

"Come on baby, you can't be sleepy already."

She looks at her cell. "It's after 2 in the morning."

"We're adults—" Just then he hears a noticeable voice. "Is that Nouvel?"

"Who?"

"Xerses' sister."

Meadowlynn looks around the beach. "I don't see anyone."

"Over there," he points.

"Put your hand down. Why do you care?"

"No reason. It's just strange seeing her out this late."

"She's a big girl. Clearly out with her man."

"I know, but she's a *good girl.*"

"Don't look all that good to me."

"I'm going to say hi."

Meadowlynn pulls him. "Are you crazy? Leave her alone."

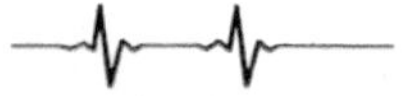

"Do you like her?" Meadowlynn screams, when they arrive back in the house.

"Who? Nouvel? No. Why?"

"Could've fooled me."

"Baby please, I'm here with you. Otherwise, I'd be with some other chick."

"Wow, that makes me feel *special.*"

"Hey, you know who I was before we hooked up. Don't do that, cuz I'll drop you just as fast as the other chick who changed up on me."

"Sorry, it's just… your body language was different when you saw her."

"Nouvel is stuck up. I won't waste my energy trying to get with a girl like her. I have you and I'm happy."

"You can't even admit that you have feelings for her."

"I don't care about her," Kage snaps.

"Very defensive, Mr. Hunter. Are you sure?"

"You know what… I'm going for a walk. Don't wait up," he says, slamming the door behind him.

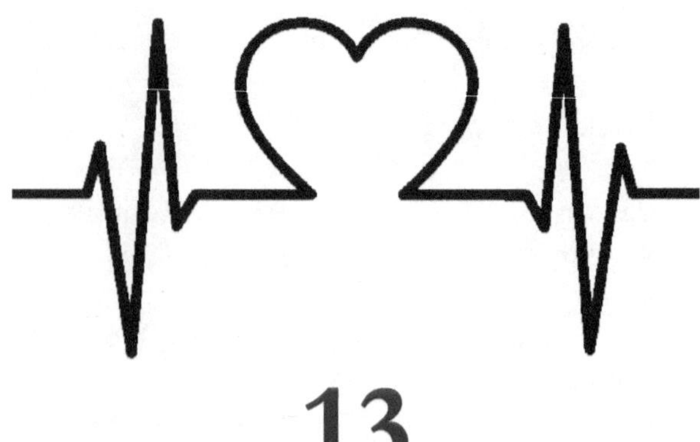

13

"What time did you get in?" Meadowlynn asks, walking out to the patio.

"Came back around 5. Slept in the guest bedroom."

"I'm sorry I flipped out earlier."

He kisses her forehead. "No need to apologize. It's not that serious."

"It is for me. I'm starting to fall for you, Kage. I can't fathom you liking another girl."

"*Fall for me?* We haven't been dating that long."

"I'd say two months is pretty long."

"I thought we were having fun."

"You're my boyfriend. And I love you."

"Look Meadowlynn, I only agreed to the *titles* because you were getting on my nerves. As far as I'm concerned, you're my long-term *flavor*, if you catch my drift."

"WOW! JUST WOW!" She punches his chest.

"Ouch!" he flinches, jokingly. "That's the kind of fierceness I love. And you do it so well… in the bedroom."

"After all this time, is that all I am to you?"

"Meadow, Meadow, we had this discussion already. We fulfill each other's needs *exclusively*. No feelings. Remember?"

"Yes, but—"

"No buts, you agreed. Or I will end this."

"So," she sobs, "you don't love me?"

"I'm 18. What do I know about love?"

"I can't believe you. You're just going to string me along?"

"Again, did you forget our deal?"

"No, but it can change. I want more." She pulls him close.

He kisses her.

"You feel that?" Meadowlynn inquires.

"Yes, and I'm *ready* to go."

"KAGE!"

"Either we're going to do it, or I'm taking you home."

"This is supposed to be a weekend of studying."

"Monday morning. Weekend's over. We can do a quickie before we head back."

"No Kage, I want more."

"Pack your bags," he grunts. "This is OVER!"

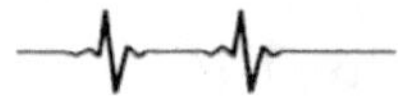

When they arrive in Meadowlynn's dorm room, Kage drops her bag on the floor. "I guess this is goodbye."

"No goodbye. Let's do it now."

"Meadowlynn please. We don't want the same thing."

She nods. "Yes, I do. I want you Kage. Take me now. Have your way with me."

"You sure?"

"Shhhh! Shhhh! No talking…"

Kage strips and makes his way to Meadowlynn's bed.

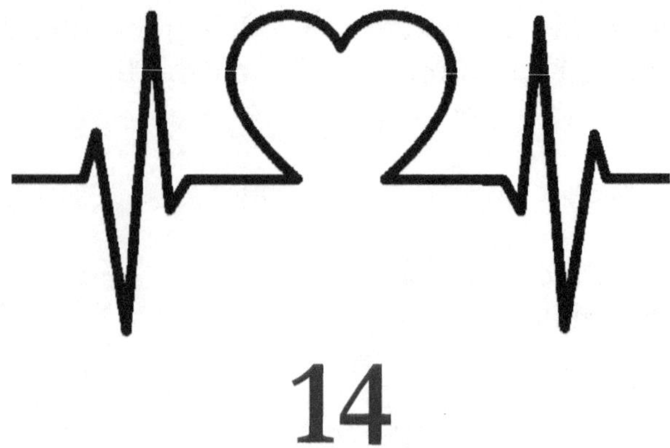

14

Kage's Epitome XX Series 1 hits the 80mph mark as he strums along with the car radio. That was the best sex he'd had in a long time. Meadowlynn definitely wanted him and he loved that.

Just then, he notices his picture on a billboard. The car jerks. "WHAT THE—"

STAY AWAY FROM
KAGE HUNTER.
HE HAS HIV!

He punched the steering wheel, letting out a loud beep. A woman walking her dog, stops.

"Are you okay?"

"What?" Kage grunts.

"Are you feeling okay? Should I call an ambulance?" She looks up at the billboard. "Wait— Is that you?"

"Look lady, I'm not in the mood!"

The woman laughs out loud. "You must've done something stupid for that to happen." She continues to laugh, as she walked away.

Exhaling profusely, Kage racked his brain trying to figure out who'd broadcast such lies. Although he was no virgin, he was careful. He used protection with his conquests. Now no woman would want to come near him.

This is the single WORST thing ANY player could see. Who did this?

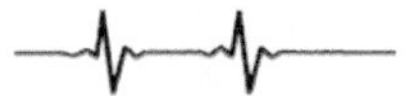

"How was the weekend?" Xerses asks, when Kage enters the dorm.

"Man, I'm in serious trouble."

"What happened?"

Kage shows him a picture of the billboard.

Xerses snickers. "Shows you right ***Mr. Player***. I told you to be careful with these girls."

"You know who did this?"

"Aside from the girl you brought to this apartment, I don't keep tabs on your sexcapades. As a matter of fact, the less I know, the better."

"I'm trying to figure out who'd do this… Hold on—" He picks up his cell. "Slow down, babygirl. You gotta let me explain. It's not true. WHAT?! Oh come on." Kage clicks his phone off. "Great, now my girl broke up with me. Said she cannot date someone with a STI."

Xerses laughs.

"This isn't funny. My rep is ruined."

"You did that on your own. What are you going to do?"

"I gotta get that billboard down. I can't have my name plastered all over town. I'm going to be a doctor someday."

"**NOW** you're thinking about your future?" Xerses quips.

"I don't need a lecture from you. I have to fix this. Really hope it doesn't go on social media."

"Too late," Xerses replies, showing him a post. "You're trending."

Kage smacks his forehead. "I have to lie low until it blows over."

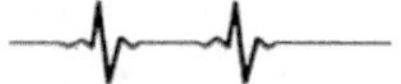

11:12PM

"Did you get my present?"

"Who is this?" Kage counters.

"The girl you gave HIV."

"Ember?"

"Yes."

"You know that's a lie. I always use protection."

"Protection means nothing."

"What are you talking about?"

"You **ruined** me, Kage."

"How?"

"Our arrangement was keeping me on top of my studies. Now I can't even function."

"I really don't care about your feelings right now. Your stunt ruined MY LIFE and FUTURE."

"Why are you mad at me, baby?" Ember cries. "I'll fix it. I promise. Please, just take me back."

"Are you deaf? I DO NOT want you!" He hangs up the phone.

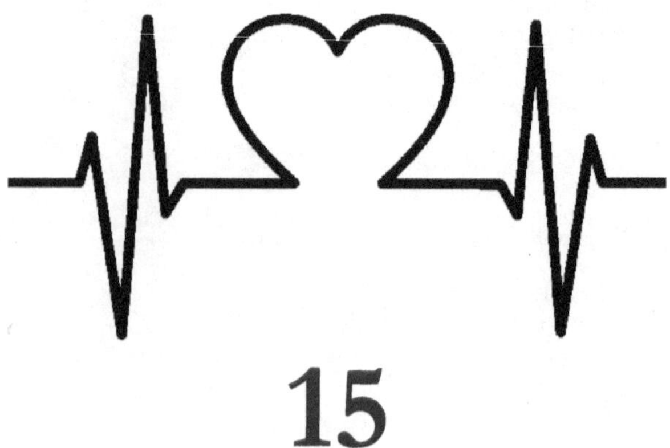

15

Semester Two

"Let's get out of here," Kage whispers.

Just then a girl walks up and slaps Kage. "Get off my friend."

"What's wrong?" his dance partner asks. "Can't you see I'm dancing?"

"Don't you know who that is?"

"No!" the girl shrugs.

"KAGE HUNTER. HE HAS HIV," her friend yells.

"Ewww... You have HIV!" his partner screams.

"It's a lie. Please, let's get out of here," Kage begs.

The girl's friend pushes him away. "Leave her alone you creep."

Why is this still happening?

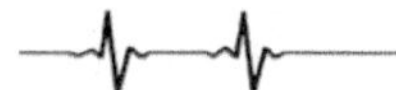

Kage walks to the balcony, holding his head in frustration.

"You okay?" Nouvel asks.

He looks at her. "Why are you talking to me?"

"You look like you can use a friend."

"We're not friends."

"You're my brother's friend. Close enough."

"What do you want, Nouvel? I don't need your pity. Your friend ruined my life."

"So, you're punishing me? Wow, mature much!"

Rayce clears his throat. "You know this guy?"

"Xerses' roommate," Nouvel introduces.

"Oh cool. Nice to meet you man."

Kage nods.

That's her boyfriend? She could do so much better.

"Let's go inside," Rayce says.

"See you later," Nouvel waves to Kage.

Rayce taps a mic. "Can I have everyone's attention please. Thanks for coming to my party. As you all know, in a few months I'll be graduating and what better way to end my university life than by doing this…" He takes Nouvel's hand. "I know you've been wondering why I've been acting so weird lately... Baby, we've been together for almost two years and I know that life without you will be meaningless. Although we're still young, I want to present you with this promise ring. Promise me that on the day of your graduation, you'll marry me."

Kage stares at Nouvel in shock. *Say no!*

"Yes, of course," Nouvel squeals.

The party goers cheer them on.

Kage takes a shot glass from a waitress, downing its contents. He walks out of the party…

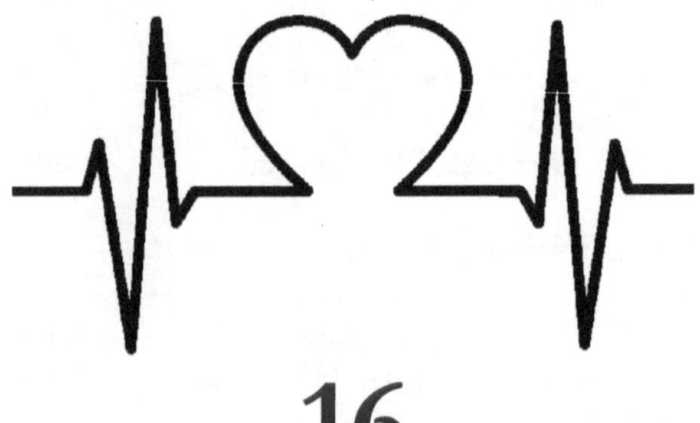

16

The Next Day

"Come on, come on," a girl says, beating on the vending machine.

"Take it easy. That doesn't work," Kage says.

"And you are?"

"You don't know me? Guy from the billboard?"

"Is that some sort of slang?"

Kage scans the girl, noting her features. *Jomivian genes.* "Wow, I've never seen a girl with lilac hair and silver eyes. You're really beautiful."

"I bet you use that line on every girl you meet."

"So you do know me," he chuckles.

"Can't say that I do. This is my first semester."

He is stunned. "Kage Hunter."

"Marwa Atherton."

"Nice to meet you, Marwa."

"Well, are you going to get me a *Blitz* or just stand there staring at my hair?"

"Oh, umm," he stutters. "Of course."

"Lunch?"

"Sure," Kage nods. "On me."

"Obviously," she scoffs.

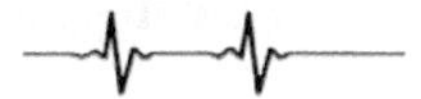

Oyster Bisque
roasted Pacific oysters
14.00

Island Salad
mixed greens, tangerine slices, crushed almonds, dried cranberry, raspberry basil vinaigrette
8.00

Honeysuckle Short Ribs
17.00

King Crab Legs
22.00

Potato Lasagna Croquettes
10.00

"You like it?" he asks.

"I've been to nicer places," Marwa shrugs.

"Oh wow, ouch!"

"So, what's your major?"

"Anesthesiology. Yours?"

"Public Health Policy."

"Hi, welcome to *Glass Oyster*, may I take your order?" a waitress asks.

"Sure, ladies first," Kage says.

"I'll have the *Potato Lasagna Croquettes*, *Honeysuckle Short Ribs*, and *Lavish Lemon Fresca* to drink… Extra ice please."

"And you, sir?"

"Same thing the lady's having."

The waitress smiles. "Your order will be out shortly."

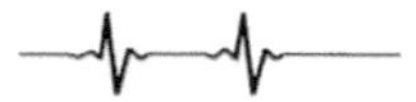

Kage laughs out loud.

"It's not funny," Marwa snickers.

"I haven't heard that joke before."

"It's not a joke. It really happened to me."

"I'm sorry Marwa, that was a funny story."

"Why are you still single?"

He rubs his neck. "I'm ashamed to say."

"Tell me, I won't judge."

"I've been busy. I don't want to get too deep into it."

"You're a player?"

"I was."

"Really?" Marwa stares at him.

"I'm trying to be better."

"What's the purpose of this date?"

"I want to get to know you better," Kage admits.

"I'm not your type."

"What's your type?"

"A guy who is faithful. I don't tolerate cheating."

"I would never cheat on a girl like you."

Marwa laughs. "I've lived all over the world and met a lot of guys and they **all** say the same thing. So excuse me if I don't believe you."

"Give me a chance and I promise you… you won't regret it."

"This lunch has been great, but I don't want you to change your ways just to be with me. Maybe we can try being friends."

"Are you serious?"

Marwa nods.

"Wow, you're the second girl to turn me down."

"Hmmm. Who's the first?"

"She doesn't matter," Kage scoffs.

"I'm ready to go when you are."

"Check please," he calls out to the waitress.

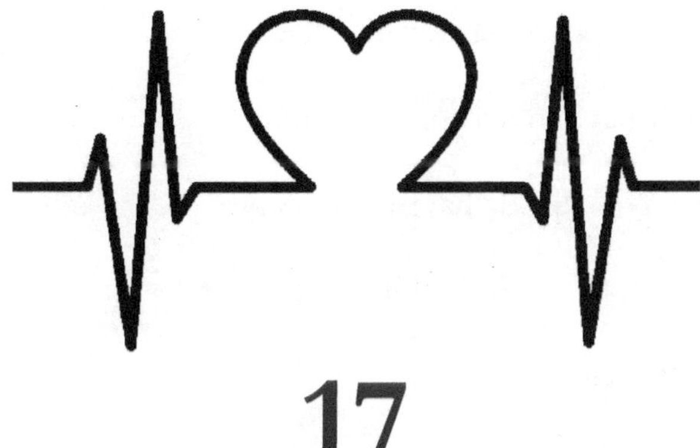

17

May

Kage and Marwa walk through the park. Suddenly, he takes her hand.

"It's been over five months, when are you going to agree to go out with me?"

"I just want to focus on school. I didn't come here for a boyfriend."

"Marwa, we've been hanging out for months. You know that I like you. Yet, you refuse to give me a chance."

"That's why you've been hanging out with me? To check me off some list?"

"No, it's not like that at all."

"I have to tell you something."

"You already have a boyfriend?" Kage sighs.

"Not that. Something important."

"I'm all ears."

"I'm a virgin—"

"Explains a lot."

"That's your response?"

"Marwa, I wasn't joking. I don't want to just *get with you*, I really want to be with you. You're a great girl. I enjoy our study sessions. You see me for me and don't judge me based on my past. I like you. I'd be a fool not to try."

She gives him an eye. "We'll see how it goes. I'm not making any promises though."

Kage grins. "That's all I'm asking."

"Okay, okay, calm down."

"You've just made me really happy."

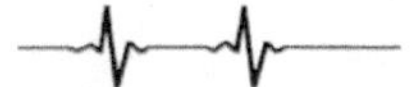

"I thought you moved out already," Kage says, entering his dorm room.

"Graduation isn't until next week."

Kage holds a match in his hand.

"Is that your ***Conquest Book***?"

"I'm a changed man."

"You're burning it? No way!" Xerses says.

"Marwa agreed to give me a chance and I don't want to mess things up."

"Be still my heart," he chuckles. "I never thought I'd see the day. Kage Hunter a changed man."

"I thought Nouvel was the dramatic one in the family?"

"I have my moments."

"Whatever man. So, what's next for you? Moving back home?"

"I got a job offer in Paxos."

"You're going to get a Greek wife?"

"At least you didn't talk about sex," Xerses chuckles.

"I didn't get you at first, but I can see how it is important for you to have one woman."

"Awww, thanks man."

Kage laughs. "Your sarcasm is next level."

"Are really going to burn the book?"

Kage tosses the book in the sink and lights the match.

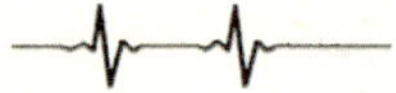

"Thanks for inviting me to your friend's graduation."

"Xerses is cool. I'm going to miss that nerd."

"Are you crying?"

"No," Kage scoffs.

"Awww," Marwa coos. "That's so sweet…" She pauses.

"What's wrong?"

"Why is that girl staring at you?"

Kage looks over to see Ember. "She's no one."

Ember walks up to them. "Kage."

"Hi Ember," he waves. "This is my friend, Marwa."

She glares at Marwa. "Mhmmm. I'm surprised that you're at graduation today."

"I came to support Xerses."

"I didn't know you two were so close."

"He was my roommate."

Marwa clears her throat.

"Well, I hope you enjoy your afternoon," Kage continues.

"Are you coming to the graduation party at the frat house?" Ember asks.

Kage shrugs. "I'm not sure. We're leaving."

"That was awkward," Marwa whispers. "One of your exes I presume?"

"We had something."

"Just how many girls did you have ***something*** with?"

"I probably shouldn't answer that."

"If you want us to be together, I need to know these things. Do you know how embarrassing it is to walk around and have girls just staring at you?"

"No need to worry about that. Those days are over."

"The past doesn't remain silent because you've ***changed***, Kage."

"What do you want me to do? Go apologize to all the girls I've been with?"

"I can't tell you how to make amends. I just know that I don't want to be a laughingstock."

Kage looks into her eyes. “Marwa, I promise, I won’t hurt you. Since we’ve been talking, I’ve been celibate.”

“Do you want a trophy for being a decent human being?”

“Why are you giving me such a hard time?”

“Kage, you’re not ready to settle down. You’re 19. I want to be in a relationship that’s leading to marriage.”

He gasps.

“Exactly… You’re not ready for a girl like me.”

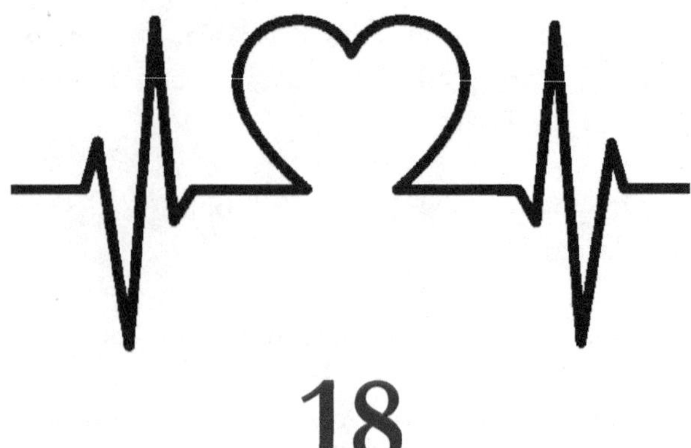

18

"Do you want to spend the summer with me?" Kage asks.

"I have plans."

"Marwa, come on. Why are you playing these games? I know that you like me."

"Did I say that?"

"What are you getting out of making me suffer?"

Marwa rolls her eyes. "Please. The first time in your life you haven't had sex and you think you're going to die?"

"I'm not talking about sex. I want to be in a relationship with you."

"Are you ready for marriage?"

"Uh—"

"Then my answer is still no."

"You want to be married at this age?"

"No. What I'm saying is that I don't want to enter into a relationship until I'm ready for marriage. I have three more years in university. I don't need the distraction of a potential heartbreak."

"Why do you assume that I'm going to hurt you?"

"It's inevitable. That's what happens at our age."

"You're judging me based on a stereotype?"

"You were a **player**, Kage."

"Thanks a lot. I thought you were nonjudgmental, but I guess I was wrong."

"I'm sorry. I just don't want to get hurt. Of course I have feelings for you. But I need to protect myself."

"I'm not going to hurt you."

Marwa sighs.

Kage hugs her. "I will do whatever it takes to prove how genuine I am."

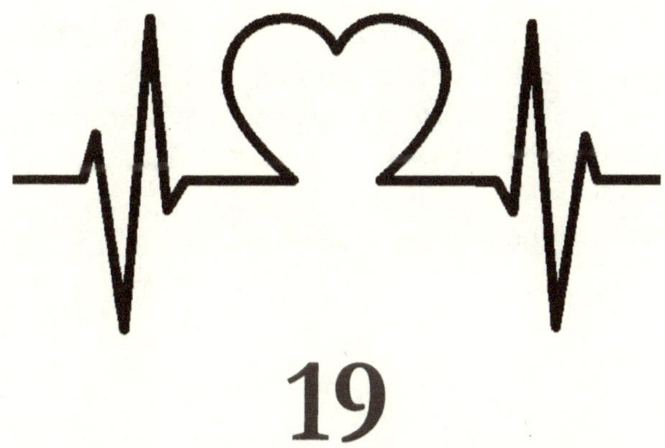

19

"Good night," Kage says, kissing Marwa's cheek.

"Are you going to come in?"

"No, I respect you too much."

"You've never seen the inside of my dorm."

"I value our friendship."

"Nothing is wrong with you coming inside."

"Look Marwa, I don't want to just come in and *hang out.* I know your stance and I respect that."

"I can handle myself. Nothing will happen."

"I'm physically attracted to you. Not gonna pretend. Just being around you drives me crazy. Self-control is hard, but I've been doing it since we met."

Marwa touches his face. Suddenly, she kisses him.

"What was that for?"

"I just wanted to get it out the way."

"Friends don't kiss."

"Maybe I want more," Marwa replies.

"Don't mess with me," Kage counters.

"I'm serious. We've been friends for about nine months and I trust you. I know you like me, but you haven't made a move. I think that we can move from friendship to a romantic relationship… ONLY if you agree that marriage is in our future."

"Yes Marwa."

"Do you agree to **everything**?"

Kage nods. "Yes, romance, marriage, the whole nine yards."

"Okay then, we're officially boyfriend and girlfriend."

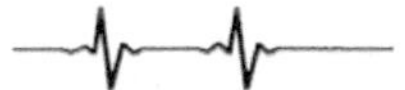

Two Weeks Later

"I can't take this from you," Marwa declines. She hands Kage a key.

"Please Marwa, I want you near me. This apartment is in a central location. You're my girl and I want to do nice things for you."

"An apartment though? That's big."

"I'm not asking you to move in with me. Just want to make sure that my girl is safe and near."

"Okay, Kage. But don't think that means you'll ever be spending the night."

Kage holds his hands up, innocently. "I wouldn't dream of it."

Taking the key from his hand, Marwa opens the door. A tear falls on her cheek, as she takes it all in. "Thank you Kage. It's beautiful."

He kisses her. "Anything for my girl."

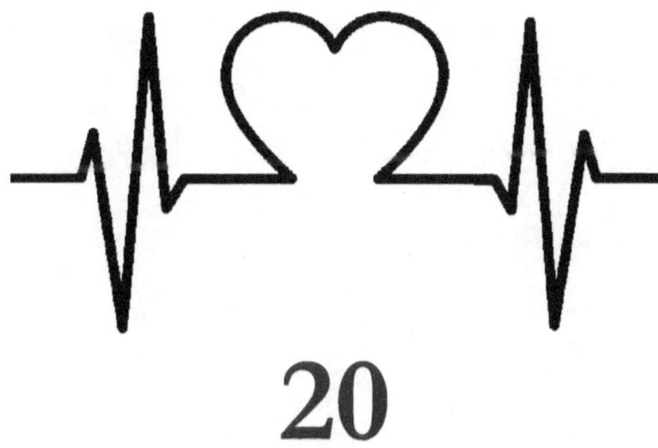

20

February

"Where are you taking me?"

"Shhh, don't ask questions," Kage replies.

Marwa gives him a side eye. "Kage, you know I'm not in the mood for any shenanigans."

"Me? ***Shenanigans?***" he chuckles.

"Boy, stop playing."

He kisses her cheek. "I wanted to show you something."

"I hope it's not a proposal."

"Proposal? Girl, you just accepted my relationship request."

"Whatever," she scoffs. "Then what is it?"

"Read this."

She hesitantly takes the paper from him.

GRAND SIERRA ISLA UNIVERSITY

Apertae mentes. Creatio futurorum.

Congratulations!

You have been directly admitted to the GSIU Abroad program. You meet the admittance criteria and it has been determined that you have the qualifications to succeed in a study abroad setting. Below is a general idea of what you should expect in the coming days.

ACCEPTANCE EMAIL

Within several days of notifying GSIU Abroad of your admission, you will receive an acceptance email with important information. Be sure to check your email (including spam and junk folders).

ACCESSING YOUR *GSIUAbroad* ACCOUNT

You will be able to access your online pre-departure information and forms. Use the login details provided. Be sure to carefully read the forms and be mindful of the due dates for various forms, including:

_**Form of Agreement and Waiver** - failure to submit this document by the due date will result in your housing information being withheld.

_**Medical Report** - this must be completed and submitted to your Abroad Advisor before departure.

DEPARTURE PACKET

Before the program commences, you will receive a final email with a program calendar outlining relevant program dates (including holidays and breaks), as well as any additional information or program changes.

If you do not receive any of the above mailings, please contact your GSIU Abroad Advisor. Once again, congratulations!

Grand Sierra Isla University
88 Heritage Passage, Trinity, Grand Sierra Isla

Phone: *88-00-20-8800
Email: GSIU@studyabroad.gsiu.si
Web: www.gsiu-studyaboad.edu.si

"I don't understand," Marwa whispers.

"They chose me, Kage Hunter, to be part of a medical study abroad program in a few weeks. It's in Argentina."

"You're leaving?"

He wipes a tear from her cheek. "Don't cry. It won't be for long. Just from the beginning of April to the end of August."

"Kage, four months is a long time."

"Ohhhh, you're gonna miss the Hunter, huh?"

"This isn't funny," she says between muted sobs.

"I thought you'd be happy for me," he snaps. "Sophomores don't get chosen for this program. My GPA is what got me in. Aside from what everyone thinks of me, I don't play with my schoolwork."

"Just hearts?"

Kage walks to kitchen and pours a glass of water. He guzzles the contents. "You're the last person I expected to behave this way."

"How am I behaving? Am I not allowed to miss you?"

"I didn't even leave yet. What are you really afraid of, Marwa?"

"That you're going to meet some foreign girl and forget all about me."

He gently takes her hands. "Marwa, I worked so hard to even get you to agree to a first date with me. Do you really think I'd jeopardize that for some *foreign girl*? You're the one I want. I see you in my future, long term… as my wife. Please stop thinking negative. We don't need that kind of vibe in the atmosphere."

Marwa continues crying.

"Okay, tell you what. No more study abroad talk. Let's go on a date. I know just the place."

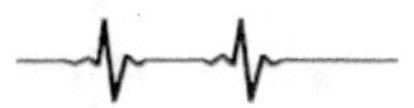

Cannelloni Di Pollo
pollo, condimento Trini, parmigiano, salsa speciale
18.00

Alfredo
pasta in salsa di burro, panna e parmigiano
16.00

Lasagne Di Verdure
carote, cipolle, condimento verde, parmigiano, formaggio cheddar
12.00

Cannelloni ai Frutti di Mare
ripieno di pesce e besciamelle con salsa di gamberi e pomodoro
24.00

Panna Cotta
speciale della casa
10.00

Gelato
sapore del giorno
4.00

Tiramisu
savoiardi, mascarpone, espresso, vaniglia
8.00

Torta di Cioccolato
cioccolato con fondente alla vaniglia
7.00

"Hunter, party for two."

"Ah yes, welcome Mr. Hunter," the waiter greets.

"Now this restaurant is fancy. Smells lovely. What type of food do they serve?"

"I'm surprised that you're impressed, Ms. Atherton. Nothing impresses you."

Marwa scoffs. "Hey, I gotta give credit where it's due. This is the nicest restaurant you've taken me thus far."

"Ouch!" he laughs. "So, all those rooftop rendezvous were mediocre?"

"They were all Starr Islands cuisine. I love our food, don't get me wrong. But, it's nice to try new flavors."

"This is authentic Trini-Italian food. It's a combination of the owners' heritage. It recently opened. Friends of my parents, I thought we'd try it out."

"Aren't they Mr. and Mrs. Popular?"

Kage laughs. He pulls out her chair.

"Thank you, kindly," Marwa blushes.

A few minutes later, a woman taps his shoulder.

"Hey Kage. I haven't seen you in a long time. You'd think we attend different universities."

"Nouvel, wow. It's been a while. How are you?"

"I'm good, waiting for Rayce."

"Ah, the boyfriend."

"Soon to be fiancé."

"Oh yeah," he scoffs, "your graduation promise."

"You remembered?"

"No one can forget such a ***grand gesture***," he teases.

"Brilliant acting skills," she claps.

"Why don't you join us, while you wait for him?"

"Really? No, I couldn't impose."

"It's no bother, right Marwa… Marwa?" He looks around. "Nouvel, wait here a minute."

"Sure," she smiles.

"Are you crazy?" Marwa snaps.

"What did I do?" he shrugs.

"Why do you think it's appropriate to invite **another woman** to *wait with us*? The restaurant has a lobby!"

"She's just an old friend."

"First time I've heard of her."

"What are you talking about? She was at Xerses' party."

"I. DON'T. CARE!"

"Since when are you so insecure?"

"EXCUSE ME?" Marwa scoffs.

"I didn't stutter," Kage retorts.

"You have some nerve. Did you have sex with her?"

"Really Marwa, really? After all we've been through, you're throwing this back in my face?"

"I told you I want to know all the girls or women you slept with. I don't want anyone laughing behind my back."

"I already gave you my phone with the names and numbers of all the women I've been with."

"You didn't answer my question," she exhales, angrily.

"No, I didn't have any contact with Nouvel, that would be construed as a sexual encounter."

"Ohhhh, I get it, she's the first girl who turned you down…"

"Can we not talk about her? We're on a date."

"Yet she's sitting **with** us. I wanna go home."

"What? We just got here."

"Kage, I'm serious. Take me home."

"You know what," he scoffs. "I'm not doing this with you. You chicks—"

"I'm a **chick** now, huh!"

"Let me finish. You chicks allllways want a good guy, yet when we try you shut us down. What's the POINT?" He throws his hands in the air and walks away.

"DON'T YOU DARE WALK AWAY FROM ME KAGE HUNTER!"

"Keep your voice down," he hushes.

"Are you gonna take me home or not?"

"I don't want to be around you right now. I'll order you a ***Rapid*** and you can go home by yourself. I'm not playing any games. I came to eat and that's exactly what I'm going to do…"

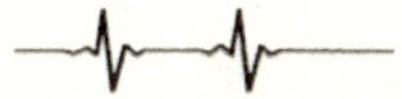

"Where'd your girlfriend go?" Nouvel asks, when Kage returns to the table.

"She wasn't feeling well."

"Come on, Kage, she looked upset."

"Doesn't matter. So—"

"Hey babe, sorry I'm late," Rayce greets.

"It's okay. I was just chilling here. You remember Kage."

"Sup!" Rayce rolls his eyes. "Our table's ready."

"Later Kage."

"Bye Nouvel," he sighs.

I need to fix things with Marwa...

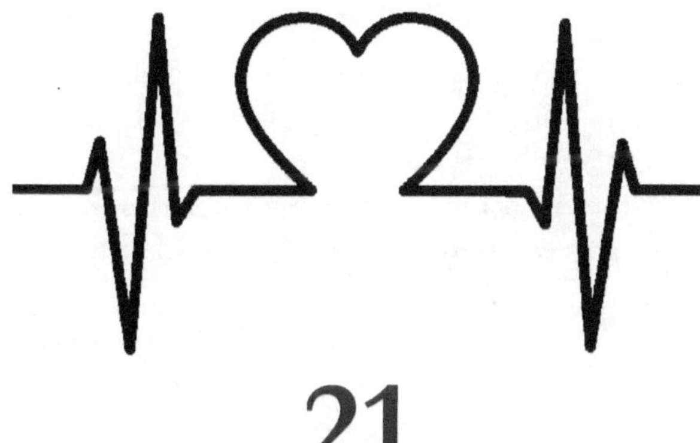

21

"I can't believe the day is here already."

"I'm going to miss you so much, Marwa."

"Are you excited?"

"Meh, it's school."

"Oh come on, you make it seem as though you don't care about school, yet you have the highest GPA in your program."

"I'm a smart and handsome man."

"That you are," she giggles.

"Do you think you'll be able to join me over the summer?"

"I can't."

"Why not?"

"Did you forget I have my internship? May not be as exciting as studying abroad, but…"

"No comparison. I just wanted you near," he replies.

"Well, we have our video calls. And you did agree that we'll talk every day. I think we'll be good. I gotta prepare myself to be a doctor's wife."

"Ahhh, my girl's thinking ahead."

Marwa blushes.

The ***Rapid*** driver announces their arrival.

"Thanks man," Kage says, as he opens Marwa's door.

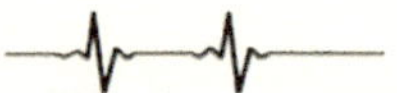

"How many checking in?" the ticket agent asks.

"Just one," Kage answers.

Marwa sighs in the background.

"My flight leaves in two hours. Let's go to the lounge until it's boarding time."

"I can't go in there without a ticket."

"Marwa, Marwa, don't you trust me?"

Silence.

"I'll take that as a *hesitant yes*," he quips.

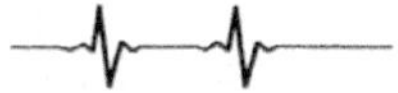

"What's going on?" Marwa asks, looking around at the beautifully decorated lounge.

"Come on, there's much to see."

"I've been to airport lounges before and none of them ever looked like this."

"Keep walking…"

"Kage, what's going on?"

He takes her hand, "Marwa Atherton, I've enjoyed these last few months with you. I don't want it to end. Because of you I've laid down my player's card, burned my black book, cancelled all memberships, and ignored every female that passed in my eyesight. That's how much I love you. And I know that you weren't expecting this so soon, but I wanted to ask you—"

"YES!" she screams.

"You better let me finish my carefully prepared speech," Kage laughs.

"Fine, fine, go ahead…"

"As I was saying before you rudely interrupted me— Sorry," he chuckles, noting Marwa's expression. "Ahem! As I was saying, I know you weren't expecting this so soon, but I didn't want to go Argentina without knowing that I have a fiancée waiting for me when I return. With that said, Marwa Atherton, would you add to my happiness, because you know Mr. Hunter is **already** a happy man… Will you marry me?"

"Yes Kage, a billion percent yes."

Just then a saxophonist comes out and plays Marwa's favorite song.

"Is that *Pretty Memories* by *The Miseno Brothers*?" she squeals.

He nods. "Shall we dance…"

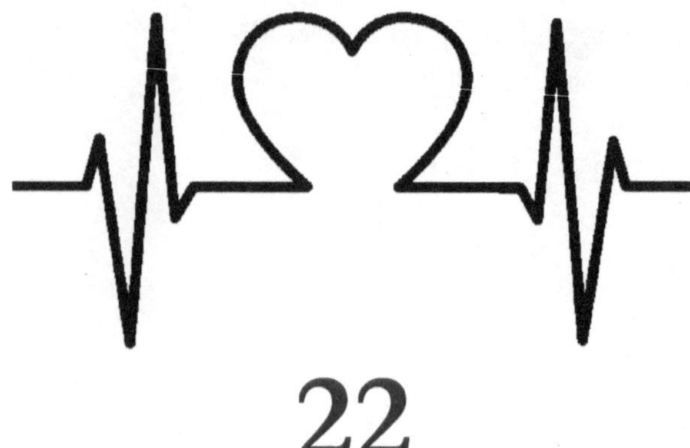

22

Argentina

Bodies moved in unison as the music permeated their beings. Kage smiles as he watches the woman control the dance floor. The way her body moved sent his mind into unknown places. When the song ended, he walked to the bar.

"¿Puedo tener una tempestad perfecta, por favor?" he asks in Spanish.

"One *Perfect Tempest* coming up," the bartender announces.

"Oh, you speak English?" Kage chuckles, nervously.

The man nods.

"Can I have what he's having?" the female dancer asks.

"Nice moves out there," Kage smiles.

"Huh?"

"Your tango moves. One of the best I've ever seen."

"You're not from here, are you?"

"The name's Kage Hunter."

"Brynn."

"Last name?"

"I don't do those."

"Noted."

"Do you know how to tango?" Brynn asks.

"I'm no pro."

"Come on, I'll help you out," she winks.

Kage downs his drink and meets Brynn on the dance floor.

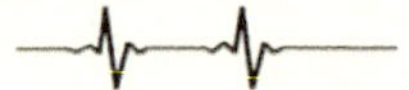

"Finally. How are you babes?" Marwa giggles.

"Hey sweets, it's been an adjustment. Sorry I didn't call you yesterday. I was dealing with jetlag."

"No problem. Met any friends?"

"I have something to tell you. I don't want there to be any secrets between us."

Her face falls flat.

"I went to a bar and danced with someone."

"Okay, was she pretty?"

"What does that matter?" he retorts.

"Was she pretty? No man is gonna be that honest if he wasn't attracted to the woman."

"Didn't notice. The place was dim."

Marwa claps sarcastically. "That's rubbish! Dim my foot."

"Anyways, um, after we finished dance, she uh—"

"TELL ME!"

"She kissed me."

"Did you enjoy it?"

"What? No!" Kage snaps.

"Good answer. Okay. Thanks for letting me know."

"You're not mad?"

"Of course I am," she scoffs. "But arguing while you are thousands of miles away doesn't do either of us any good."

He remains silent.

"Are you gonna see her again?" Marwa prods.

"This program is intense. We only had a two-day transition period—"

"It's okay, Kage. I trust you. You haven't given me any reason not to. Just make sure to call me every chance you get."

"Yes sweets."

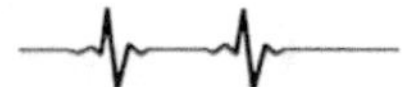

El Tambor Llamativo

"Mr. Hunter, you've been here every day since you arrived," the bartender notes.

"Montes, my man. I can't get this chick off my mind."

"What happened to your fiancée?" he says, wiping the counter.

"She's still around. This is for her."

"I don't think she'd appreciate you searching Argentina for the woman you kissed your first night here."

"Whatever, you bartenders know too much."

"Yup," Montes nods. "Enough to write books."

"You're into literature?"

"Because I'm a bartender you think I'm not educated?"

"Hey, the Hunter doesn't judge. So back to Brynn, when was the last time you saw her?"

"She comes and goes. Travels a lot."

"I didn't get much from her that night."

"Well, this isn't the most conducive place for dating."

"I told you it's not like that."

"Whatever man. Fair warning, women like Brynn aren't the *settling down* type. She's **very dangerous**."

"I don't judge."

"You may be standing in front of a judge if you hook up with a girl like her. Take it from someone who knows."

"You tapped that?"

"*Ella no es mi tipo.* But I know a few guys who've come to this bar crying over her. You seem like a cool dude, stick with your girl and leave Brynn alone!"

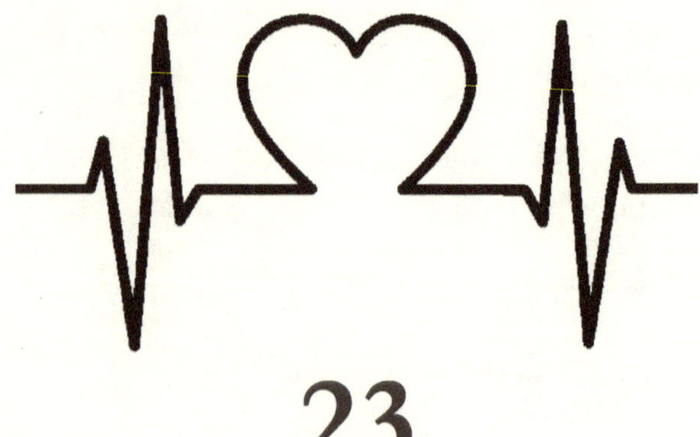

23

August

"Finallllyyyy, you're back," Marwa says, jumping on Kage.

"Now **that** is the type of welcome for a Hunter. Hey sweets. I missed you."

Marwa kisses him passionately.

"Not in front of strangers," Kage chuckles, when they pulled apart.

"Please don't leave me again. That was a hard four months."

"Harder for me."

"What do you mean?" Marwa asks.

"Doesn't matter. How are we going to celebrate my return?"

"Let's go to my place."

"Are we going to—"

"No Kage," she rolls her eyes, "we're **not** going to be having sex."

"Eh, can't blame a man for trying. I guess I really have to wait until our honeymoon."

She nods.

"Fine. I'll wait…" he teases.

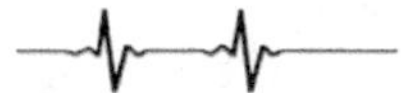

"Gonna take a shower, do you mind?" he asks when they arrive in Marwa's apartment.

"Of course not, your things are still in the drawer."

"I didn't expect it to be anywhere else," he scoffs.

"Just go shower…"

Kage kisses her forehead. "I'll be back in jiff."

"Since when do you talk like that?"

"Remember Montes?"

"The bartender?"

Kage nods. "He's from the USA, taught me a few terms."

"You already knew a lot from watching TV."

"Are you gonna let me shower or not? We'll talk after…" He heads to the bathroom.

His phone goes off and a notification pops up. Marwa reads the heading. "Hmmm, that's strange. Why would Kage's bank be calling? Is he in some kind of trouble?"

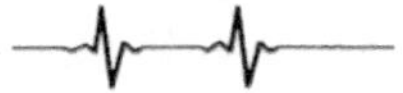

"All done," he says, wiping his hair with a towel. "What's wrong?"

"I should be asking you that. You've received eleven notifications from **Bank Teller**! The bank doesn't send that much notifications."

"Let me see that."

She hands him the phone.

A frown spreads across his face. "I'll be back later tonight okay. Gotta handle something."

"Is everything alright?"

"I used my bank card a lot in Argentina. Those notifications were alerts."

"Oh my gosh. Did someone try to steal your money?"

"That's what I'm going to find out."

"Okay, no problem. Let me know how I can help."

"Just wait here until I come back."

Marwa nods. A worried expression crosses her face.

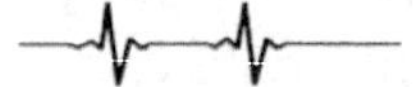

Two Hours Later

"Kage, what's going on?"

"What are you doing here?"

"This is not the bank," Marwa retorts.

"You followed me?"

"Who's she?"

The woman opens her mouth to speak, but Kage shoots her a look.

"No, no, Kage, let her talk," Marwa snaps.

"Let me explain…"

"Explain what?"

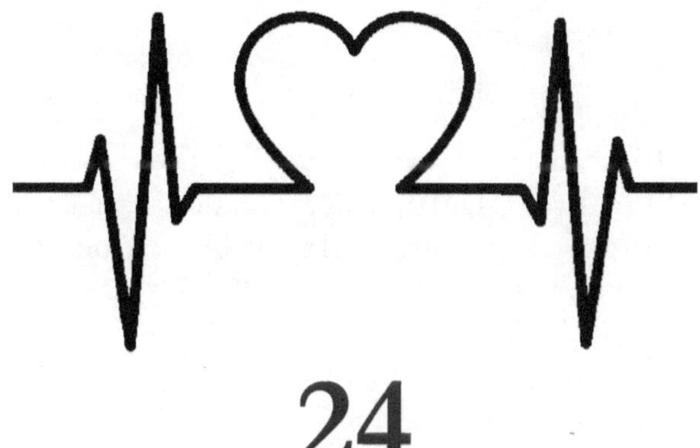

24

"HELLO! I asked you a question."

"I'm going." The woman kisses Kage. "Thanks for the money, sweets."

"WOW! The audacity. She kissed you with familiarity."

"Marwa, please let me explain."

"I'm all ears."

Five minutes of silence pass.

"Still waiting," Marwa says, tapping her wrist.

"She's an escort," he reveals.

"Come again?"

"You know… an *escort*."

"I'm not DUMB, Kage. I know what an escort is. I was just giving you a chance to come up with a better answer."

"I have needs."

"N-needs? Oh, you mean **sex**?" Marwa laughs manically. "I knew that you couldn't keep it in your pants. You really a true player for real, aren't you Mr. Hunter?"

"I tried Marwa; I really did."

"For how long? ***Two seconds***?" She begins to cry.

"Please don't cry. I'm sorry. I really am. I guess this is goodbye then."

"You're not getting off that easily."

"What else is there to talk about? I've already shared my secret. I don't need the condescending lecture. Heard it many times before."

"How long have you been seeing her?"

"Please, just leave it," Kage pleads.

"NO! You're going to give me an answer. I deserve at least that."

"We started messing about—"

"Call it what it is," she says, poking his chest. "SEX. Say it! You've been having **SEX** for how long?"

"Fine, if that's what you wanna hear… I met her a week after I met you at the vending machine. We started having sex the day I met her."

"You have no morals. No values. What made you become this nasty specimen?"

"Don't judge me!" Kage barks.

"I know that men love sex, but you've taken it to another level. Every single female in GSIU knows KAGE HUNTER!"

"What else can I say?"

She slaps him in the face. "You have SOME NERVE. I hope some woman breaks your heart the way you've broken so many of our hearts. Better yet, I hope you **die ALONE**

AND MISERABLE! You're nothing but a **low self-esteem LOSER**!"

"Thanks for letting me know how you really feel. I thought you loved me."

"L-love? YOU have the NERVE to talk about LOVE?" Marwa laughs. "Just when I thought I knew everything about you. I wasn't aware that you were a comedian as well. What do you know about love?"

"Get it all out," he retorts.

"Don't TELL ME WHAT TO DO! You don't have any rights in my life."

"I got to see Marwa Atherton's **true colors**. Times of adversity and you've already pushed me off the cliff…"

"Are you hearing yourself? I *have neeee-ds,*" she mocks. "Now you're acting all innocent. Give me a break. All I know is that one day you will suffer the consequences for your actions. I hope **all** of your sexcapades comes rushing back to memory."

"Again, I'm sorry Marwa. I don't have anything else to say." Kage shrugs and walks away.

Marwa stands there with tears streaming down her face.

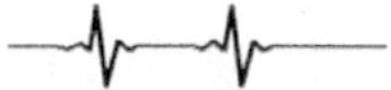

"Bravo ladies, bravo," Ember claps as she comes from behind a van.

"Was I convincing?" Marwa smirks.

"Girl, you deserve all the awards in *Vias*."

The "escort" chuckles. "Ah, Mr. Hunter doesn't know that he's been set up. Brilliant plan, Ember."

"Thanks ladies. I am so happy that you agreed to help me. It's been very hard playing this charade for over a year. With the part of virgin girl… Marwa Atherton. Thanks, cuz."

"You're welcome girlie. I can't believe he actually thinks I'm a virgin and that I go to GSIU. He never asked much about my classes. I'm not even a student there."

Ember snickers, "I think the greatest feat is you convincing him to get you an apartment in **your** name."

"Should I give it back to him?"

"Nah," all three women laugh.

"All that's coming to Mr. Hunter is his own fault." She turns to the escort. "Was he good in bed?"

The woman shrugs, "Mediocre at best. But we have a lot of money because of him."

"Thanks for all your help, Cotta."

Cotta nods. "It was hard not being able to touch the money. How'd you know when to end the charade?"

"When Marwa told me that Kage was going to Argentina, I thought a perfect end to his stupid Sophomore year would be a breakup."

"I wonder if he knows he's been swindled?" Marwa asks, softly.

"I know you had it the hardest because of your relationship. I know you fell for him, but actress' have a role to fulfill and when the curtain closes, job's done."

"I do feel sorry for him though."

Ember shoots Marwa a dirty look. "Why?"

"I think something happened that caused his negative behavior."

"Look, I DO NOT CARE about the reasons that made Kage a nasty scamp. What I do care about is laying low for a while. Love you cuz, but we can't be seen together for a while. You neither, Cotta."

They nod in agreement.

"Now, how much money do we have to divide by three?" Ember inquires.

"With today's payment… $150,000," Cotta reveals.

Ember smiles. "Hmmm, he really is rich. Alright ladies, let's go divvy up this money. Thankfully I have my connections so no one will ask about the sum…"

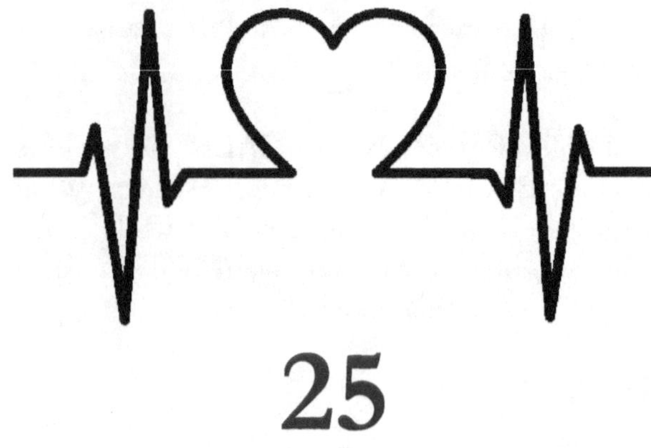

25

Junior Year

"Ladiesssssssssss of GSIU get your purses out. Make sure your bank account has money in it, because we're pleased to introduce to you the Upperclassmen, our Juniors and Seniors. The hot and sexy men of Grand Sierra Isla University. All proceeds go toward funding our new student lounge. Without further ado, are you ladies ready to **BUY. A DATE…**" the MC announces.

The women erupt in applause.

"And now we begin with the man with the highest GPA in GSIU's Anesthesiology

Department, the one we all love to hate… KAGE HUNTER!"

Blank stares fill the room.

"Come on ladies, this is for a good cause."

Silence.

Kage stands on the stage awkwardly. Someone signed him up for the auction and when he found out, it was too late. He knew that all the women on campus hated him.

Can we just get this over with? No one's gonna bid on me.

"$2,000."

All eyes turn to the woman holding the check book in her hand.

"Whoa!" the MC exclaims. "$2,000 going once… going twice… sold to the strange woman that no one seems to know."

Kage looks up to see the bidder. "Brynn?"

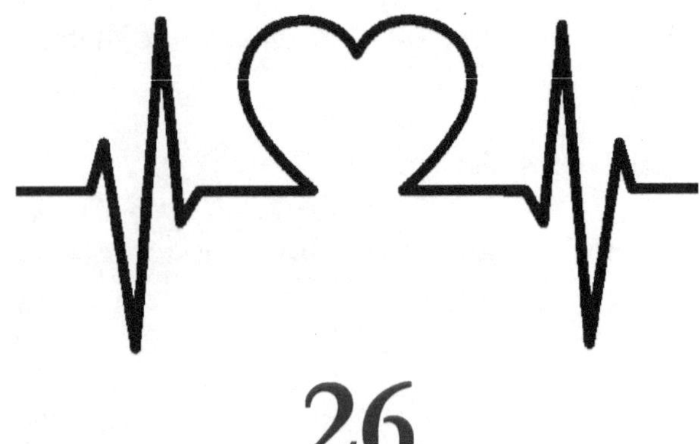

26

"What are you doing in GSIU?"

"I told you that my family is from Starr Islands."

"You told me nothing," Kage quips.

"How are you, *dance partner*?"

"It's been an interesting few weeks."

"Care to talk about it over dinner?" she asks.

"You're treating me? What for?"

"Can't an old friend treat you to dinner?"

"I only met you that one time in Argentina. And out of all the places to meet up… my university?" Kage replies.

"Here's the address to the location. I'll meet you there."

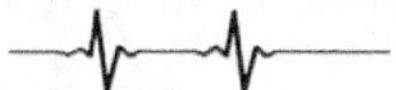

"Brynn this is an amusement park. Not exactly a place for dinner."

"Meh, dinners are overrated. I say let's eat hotdogs and go on the rides until we hurl."

"Really?" he looks perplexed.

"No silly, there's a restaurant on the grounds that I've been waiting to try for months."

Kage burps in contentment. "Excuse my manners."

"Be yourself," Brynn dismisses. "I love a man with a hearty appetite."

"Come on Brynn, tell me the truth, what are you doing here? I know you're not in university. You're at least 24 or so."

"Wow, a lady never tells her age."

"I'm not saying you look old, but I know a woman who's been around when I see one."

"What are you insinuating, Mr. Hunter?"

"I didn't stutter."

"Fine," she chuckles, "I am older than you, but we're in Starr Islands and you've been an adult for 5 years."

"Clocking my age, I see."

"No sir."

"Why are you here?"

"Truthfully?"

Kage nods.

"Nothing as exciting as you'd think… Work. I found out about the auction through the MC. She's a good friend of mine. And when she told me that you were on the list, I decided that I wanted to meet you again. You were a really good dance partner. With moves like that, I wondered if you were good at something else."

His face turns red.

"Oh, I made the Hunter blush."

"I thought the MC didn't know you?"

"She was joking… 'no one ***seems*** to know'? That's part of our ongoing joke."

"Dang, it's like all the women in Grand Sierra Isla knows me."

"What do you mean?"

"I don't wanna bore you with my life story."

"Now I'm even more intrigued," Brynn replies.

"Apparently some of the women I was having sex with plotted against me. I got swindled out of $150,000."

"Whoa, you're ballin' like that? You got money money. Why didn't you take it to the police?"

He shrugs. "I figured I deserved it for what I did. I thought my ex-fiancée was a ***nice innocent virgin***. Not knowing that she was an actress, hired by one of the chicks I used to mess with. And in between there was an escort, **also** hired by that chick. To make matters worse, my ex-fiancée was the chief conspirator's **COUSIN**. Besides, if I take this to the police my parents would find out and I'd be a dead man."

"Whoa. What a story to tell your wife someday."

"Wife! HA! I'm staying away from women. They're all liars!"

"Hmmm, this coming from a known player?"

"I see my reputation precedes me."

"You get what you deserve, I guess," Brynn shrugs.

"Wow, thanks."

"No, I'm serious. Each of us have tests that we have to go through until we ***get it***."

"Get what?" Kage counters.

"When you ***get it***, you'll know. The ***it*** is different for everyone."

"You're not making any sense."

Brynn laughs. "Doesn't matter. It made sense in my head."

"Do you have a sugar high?"

She chuckles.

"I think it's time for us to go."

"I'm not drunk. Calm down. Besides, I paid $2,000 for you. We're **GOING** to have a good time."

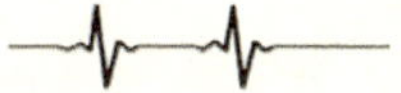

"When do you start internship?" Brynn asks, as they walked through the amusement park.

"How do you know about my internship?"

"You're a Junior in a medical program, of course there's an internship."

He shrugs, "There's been a few hospitals that has showed interest in me, but I'm not sure which to choose."

"I can help if you'd like."

"Why would you want to help me pick something as boring as an internship?"

"I know people and just thought I'd point you in the right direction. The right placement could make or break your future as a doctor," she retorts.

"I think I'm fine in that department. With my GPA I can go anywhere."

"Going anywhere and **thriving** anywhere is two different things."

"Okay Brynn, tell you what. I'm a visual learner. Why don't you create some sort of portfolio explaining the pros and cons of each hospital and I'll choose one."

"Seriously?"

"Yup," he nods. "I just want to be an Anesthesiologist. All this go between bores me."

"Hey, we all have to go through the process."

"You lost me there."

"I'll meet you at your place in the morning," Brynn volunteers. "10 sounds good to you?"

"That's good timing. I'll have breakfast ready."

"Don't get any ideas, Mr. Hunter, we're not gonna be dating."

"Dating? I heard you're bad news."

"I don't mind that title. Kage," Brynn flirts, "If I wanted you, I could have you right now."

His heart races.

"But," she says whispering in his ear, "I'd rather you sweat… See ya tomorrow."

I need a cold shower…

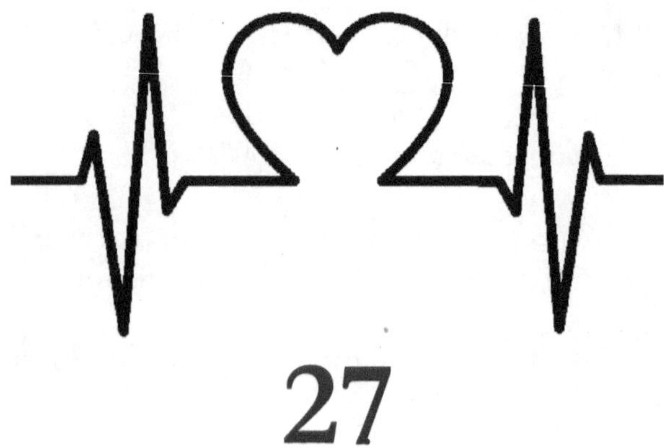

27

"Why are you wasting my time?"

"Come on Brynn, stop acting like that," Kage scoffs.

"I know it's not in the Hunter's DNA to grovel. What exactly do you want from me?"

"It's been two weeks. Why won't you let me take you out?"

Brynn laughs. "You sound so pathetic. Sorry Mr. Hunter, I'm seriously not interested in whatever plot you have to get in my bedroom."

"Tsk. You know it's not like that."

She yawns. "You bore me. Everything doesn't have to be physical. I need a **man** in my life. Not just someone who wants to *play the field.* That gets boring. I've been there, done that, and…"

"Yeah right. You're the one who flirted with me, remember? How'd you think I'd react?" Kage asks.

"Perception, perception. That's all that was. You **THOUGHT** I was flirting with you because you swear up and down the coasts of Starr Islands that **every single woman** wants you. Hate to break it to you. I really don't care. I'm accustomed to excitement. Your lines are tired. I'm sure your manhood is shriveled up at this point. If you want to hang out as friends, that's fine. But as for sex. HA! Not happening."

"That's what they all say. But my memories prove otherwise."

"GOOD. FOR. YOU," she claps sarcastically. "Do you want a biscuit? Trophy? What? What do you want? You're sounding like a total idiot just standing here trying to prove **why** we should have sex. Like, are you kidding me?"

"You know what, Brynn? Whatever. This isn't even about sex."

"Get out, I don't want you in my condo anymore."

"Don't have to ask me twice," he hisses.

Another stupid girl, who I guarantee will end up on my list. I've heard every song in the book...

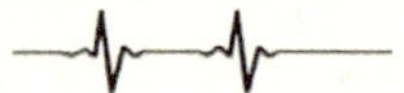

Kage slams his car door shut. He scrolls through the radio stations.

"...you've spent your entire life trying to be someone you're not. Accept Jesus Christ today and watch HIM turn your life around," the broadcaster announces.

"What foolishness?" Kage laughs. "Who is this Jesus character? Why does my life need *turning* around?"

A few minutes pass.

Do you want your daughter to marry a man like you? A still voice whispers.

Kage's eyes open wide. "Who said that?" He looks around the vehicle. "WHOA!" he says as his tires screech. "I must be more tired than I thought.

Do you want your daughter to cry every time someone breaks her heart? The voice continues.

"This is crazy." He looks at the radio. **Off.** "I didn't even drink anything strong."

Kage pulls into a gas station.

"Put $20 on pump 2."

"You okay man?" the gas station attendant asks.

"I'm fine," Kage nods.

"Looks like you saw a ghost."

"More like heard one," he mutters under his breath.

"I didn't catch that," the man replies.

"Can I have my receipt?"

The attendant hands Kage the receipt.

Moments later, Kage drives home.

Now I'm hearing voices...

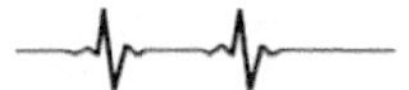

The Next Morning
Advisor's Office

"You wanted to see me, sir?"

"Have a seat, Mr. Hunter," Professor Noud replies.

"Am I in trouble?"

"Now what makes you think that you're in trouble?"

Kage' eyes shift to the other side of the room. "I'm sure that you've heard things on campus."

"It's not my job to judge students' **extra-curricular activities**. You are all adults."

"What is this about?" he snaps. "I didn't sleep well."

"You should go see the campus therapist."

"Nah, I'm good," Kage counters.

"I'm not much for small talk, so I'll cut straight to the point… Why haven't you signed up for an internship hospital?"

"I thought I had a few more weeks."

"No, Mr. Hunter," Professor Noud says, "your time is up. You have to choose a hospital by this afternoon. Internship starts next week."

Kage jumps out of the chair. "NEXT WEEK? Just how long have I been sleeping?"

"Enough with the theatrics. Make a decision and let me know. You may leave my office," the professor dismisses.

"If you walk any further, you'll wear your shoes out," Brynn smiles.

"What are you doing here?" Kage asks.

"Came to visit my friend."

"You seem to conveniently show up in the most opportune time."

"I'm not sure what you're talking about. As I said, I came to visit my friend. If you'll excuse me…"

"Wait, wait, wait, wait," Kage says, running up to her.

"Did you want something?"

"I need your help."

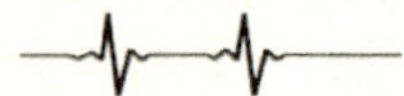

Monday

"Thanks for helping me choose my internship hospital. How'd you arrive at this particular one?"

"It was a no-brainer, I work here," she chuckles.

"I see, so basically what you're saying is, you wanna see more of the Hunter?" Kage winks.

"Don't flatter yourself. This is the best hospital on the island. Everyone knows that. And now you're going to be trained by the best."

"I'm not going to lie, I'm sort of nervous," he reveals.

"Why? Because you can't sleep your way to the top?" Brynn jabs.

"Now wait a minute. I worked really hard. I know people don't think much of me, but academically, I don't play. My parents will literally kill me if I mess things up."

"Tell me more about your parents…"

"Kage Hunter. We're ready to begin," the instructor announces.

"See you later, Brynn."

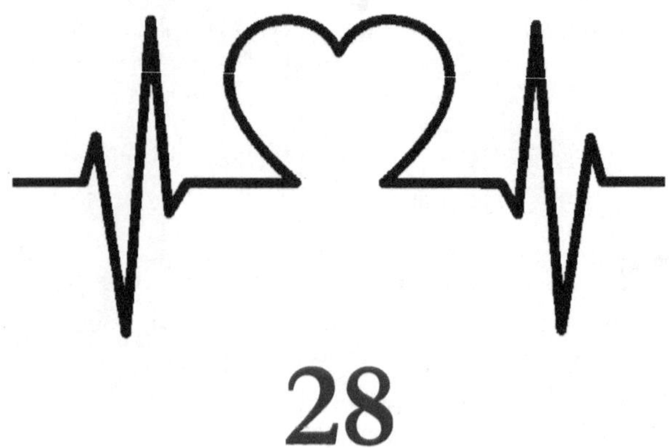

28

Brynn puts a piece of cake in Kage's mouth.

"Next question," he requests.

"An anesthesia machine is set to deliver oxygen 2 L/min, *Tacrorudin Artesonide* 2 L/min, and *Agaldizem*. After 30 minutes of stable anesthesia, what is the **most** likely cause of a **decrease** in the oxygen analyzer reading from 50% to 30%?"

"I know this, I know this," Kage taps his forehead.

"Come on, I know you can do it," Brynn encourages.

"*Tacrorudin Artesonide,* laughing gas, right?"

Brynn nods.

"Okay, the answer is... accumulation of water on the oxygen sensor membrane." He looks at her for a response.

She scans the answer key. "Mr. Hunter... you are **correct**!"

"YES!" Kage jumps in excitement.

"That was the last question."

"Thank you so much, Brynn. Do you think I'm ready for the midterm?"

"I have no doubt that you're going to ace this exam. We've been studying for three months."

"Let's go celebrate."

Brynn wrinkles her nose. "Can't."

"Why not?"

"I have a date."

"Date? With who? I didn't know you were seeing someone."

"We're not exclusive," she shrugs.

Kage pulls her in close.

"What are you doing?"

"Shhh," he counters.

"Kage, stop."

He begins to kiss her neck. "Do you really want me to stop?"

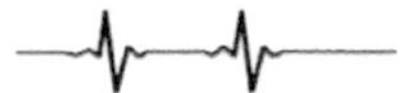

"Last night should not have happened," Brynn snaps, while putting on her clothes.

"I know you wanted me," he smirks, coming in for a kiss.

Brynn pushes him. "STOP KAGE STOP!"

"What is it?"

"This is deeper than you think. I—" Brynn's phone rings. "Sorry, I have to get this."

He watches her pace the room.

"Hello? I'm sorry. I know I should've called, but… Please stop yelling. Fine. I'll be right there."

"You okay?" Kage asks.

"I gotta go!" Brynn says, picking up her belongings.

"That was weird." He shrugs and walks over to his phone. "Well Brynn, you're officially on my conquest list." Kage heads to the shower, laughter escaping his lips.

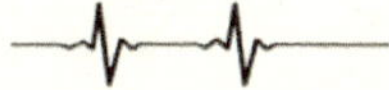

Brynn sits in the hospital lounge, biting into a sandwich.

"Can I have a piece?" Kage asks.

"Funny. How was the exam?"

"Look, Brynn, about last night—"

Brynn wipes her mouth with a napkin, then shoots Kage a look. "What are you doing?"

"I'm apologizing for last night."

"Why?" she mumbles.

"Because of the way you left. I don't want things between us to be awkward."

"You're making it awkward," Brynn counters.

"How?"

"Nothing happened last night that I didn't want to happen. We weren't drunk. Just forget it. You have another conquest for your stupid list. Whatever, it doesn't matter. That's all women are to you any way… SEX!"

"Brynn, come on, we're not like that."

"I thought you were fun." She laughs. "You're so gullible. Look Kage, I don't care. None of this matters. I have bigger things to think about than sexing a known lothario."

"If you're not mad, then why'd you storm out this morning?"

"Can we not talk about this? I have a meeting that I'm dreading. I'll see you later," she says, kissing him.

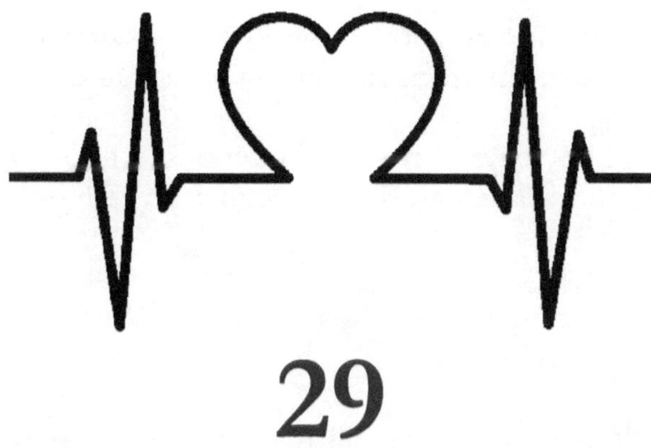

29

A Few Months Later

"We need to talk," Brynn says, as they sat on the park bench.

"I don't think I like where this is going," Kage gulps.

"I'm pregnant."

"Excuse me, come again."

"Pregnant. As in with child."

"By who?" Kage snaps. "It can't be me. I always use protection."

"Maybe you should check your ***protection*** because I'm pregnant and you're the father."

"Nah, Brynn, you're not serious. That's so cliché. Player ends up a father by the *wild card*."

"This isn't a joke, Kage. I haven't been with anyone else."

"That's what they all say. Besides, we only had sex one time."

Brynn rolls her eyes. "You have the highest GPA in the school, yet you're acting like you have a low IQ?" She kisses her teeth.

"I can't be the father of your baby. That's not in my plans."

"Just how long did you think that you'd be able to have your sexcapades before you became a father?" Brynn scoffs.

"I. ALWAYS. USE. PROTECTION. No woman is going to trap me with any child. I have plans."

"Wow, so you don't think I have plans too? You don't think this will mess it up?"

“Brynn,” Kage exhales. “Please tell me that you’re joking.”

Tears streamed down her face. “I wish.”

“Are you crying right now?”

She bursts into hysterics.

“I don’t do tears,” Kage says. He looks at her. “Brynn, please stop.”

“I didn’t want this for my life.”

“Why don’t you have an abortion?”

“ARE YOU CRAZY? I’m not murdering my child,” Brynn yells.

“It’s not a baby yet.”

She slaps him. “Don’t be stupid. From the moment your sperm went into my egg, fertilization began. It’s very much a baby from day one as it is at nine months.”

Kage grits his teeth. “How far along are you?”

“I’m around twelve weeks.”

“Okay, so what’s next?”

"I have an ultrasound appointment if you want to join me."

"I'd rather not," he declines. "Don't want to get attached to a baby that isn't mine."

Brynn pulls him. "You ARE the father and you're coming."

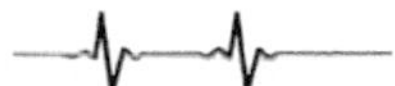

Doctor Lever, OBGYN

"Are you ready?" Dr. Lever asks.

"As I'll ever be," Brynn shrugs.

"Is this the father?"

"No," Kage coughs.

"He's in denial, so I'll say **sperm donor**," Brynn says.

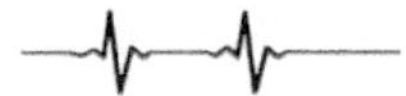

Kage stares at the screen in horror.

"Can you tell the baby's gender?" Brynn asks.

The doctor moves the transducer around Brynn's abdomen. "It looks like you're having a girl—"

"Kage, did you hear? We're having a girl…"

"I think I'm going to be sick," Kage says, bolting out of the room.

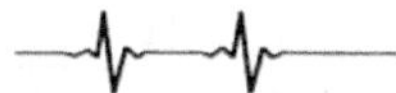

Do you want your daughter to marry a man like you?

Do you want your daughter to cry every time someone breaks her heart?

"Kage," Brynn snaps. "That was really humiliating. Even for you."

"Not now, Brynn. I need to go to the hospital," he gags.

"We **are** in a hospital. Are you okay?"

He stares at her.

Are you scared that someone may break your daughter's heart?

"What did you just say?"

"I said, *are you ready to go?* You really don't seem well. Maybe you should go see a doctor."

"No," he declines. "I just need to go home and relax. This internship has me on edge."

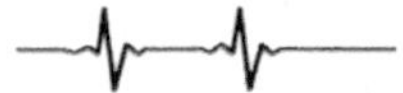

Kage's phone rings. ***It's 4AM. Who could be calling me at this hour?*** He clicks the device without looking at the screen. "Hello?"

"I'm hungry."

"Brynn?"

"Can you get me some *Lasagna Croquettes*?"

"You've gotta be joking."

"Kage, I'm hungry," she snaps.

"Brynn, I have to be in the hospital for 7AM. I'm just trying to get some sleep."

"I'm waiting," she says, hanging up the phone.

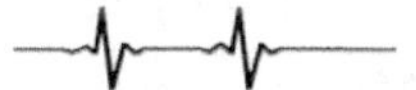

4:45AM

Kage pounded the door.

Brynn answers. "Why are you making so much noise?"

"Just take it, I need to get back to sleep."

Brynn wrinkles her nose. "I don't want that. You took too long. The craving has passed."

Anger boiled within Kage. "Brynn, you're going to **TAKE THIS AND EAT IT.** You woke me up out of my sleep to get this for you."

"You can't force a pregnant woman to eat if she doesn't want to."

"WOMAN! EAT THIS FOOD!"

"Kage, you need to go. I don't need any drama from you. I'll see you at work later…"

He balled up his fists as he screamed through the halls.

THIS CHICK IS CRAZY! I did not sign up for this foolishness...

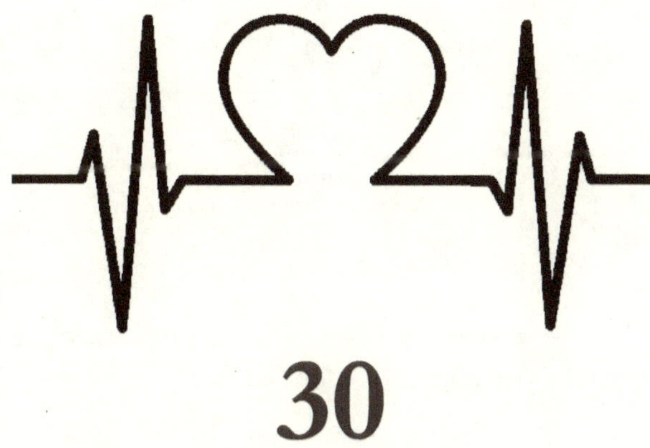

30

"Congratulations, you've now completed your internship. Mr. Hunter, the Chief would like to speak to you in his office," the instructor reveals.

Kage looks at the woman. "What for? I never met the man."

She walks up to him. "Mr. Hunter, getting placed in a hospital such as this would be most beneficial for your future. I'm sure that the Chief wouldn't call you in his office for bad news."

"Okay Professor."

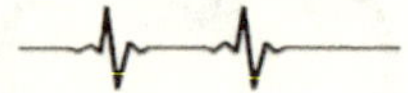

"Ah, the illustrious Kage Hunter."

"Good afternoon, sir."

"Have a seat. I'd like to formally introduce myself. The name's Chief Barclay."

Kage shakes the man's hand. "To what do I owe the pleasure?"

Chief Barclay clears his throat. "I'll just be frank with you. My hospital is the TOP hospital on this island. We only hire the **best.** And I want you on my team. Now I know that there's been many hospitals near and far contacting you. One of the beauties of studying in Starr Islands is the accelerated Med School programs. Three years of undergrad, an internship, and the SYMSBP (Senior Year Med School Bridge Program) for the students with 3.5 and above GPAs. I didn't want to tell you this before your advisor, but with your impeccable grades and well-rounded extracurricular activities, you're guaranteed to be class valedictorian in a few weeks."

"Wow! That's excellent news. I knew that I got in the program, but graduating top of the undergrad class—"

"I'd really like you to come on board, Mr. Hunter. Not trying to sway you, but I know that *Grand Sierra Medical Hospital* will be an excellent fit for you. Upon completion of med school, we'd like to offer you a residency position. You don't look like a man who's interested in ***minor details***. If you say yes today, I'll put your name in the system. We'll monitor your med school progress and when you're done, you come work for us. How does that sound?"

"Tempting, but I don't want to make a decision based on a whim. Give me until the end of the week and I'll let you know. I also need to discuss it with my advisor."

"Smart man. This is exactly why we need you on the team. No rash decisions."

Out in the hallway, Kage exhales in anger. He'd forgotten his phone in Chief Barclay's office when he overheard a conversation.

"Brynn, you shouldn't be in here," Chief Barclay snaps.

"But dad—"

Kage barges into the room. "What's going on?"

"I can explain," Brynn says.

"Explain what? The Chief is your father?"

Chief Barclay looks at Kage, perplexed. "Oh, my angel didn't tell you?"

Kage scowls at Brynn.

"Yes, the Chief's my dad," Brynn reveals.

"And when were you planning on telling me this?"

"I didn't think it mattered," she shrugs. "You got in on your own merit."

"Is this a game to you? You **used** me."

"Kage no, it's not like that."

"Then tell me, BRYNN. What is it like? This is the first I'm hearing about this. I didn't even know your last name. Even in the age of social media, I couldn't find you."

"Brynn Rizo-Barclay."

"How PERFECT for you Ms. Barclay."

"Rizo-Barclay," the Chief corrects. Rizo is her mother's name."

"What exactly was this plan of yours?" Kage asks.

"Do you want to tell him or should I?" the Chief asks Brynn. "You know I'm not much for small talk."

"Dad, please…"

"Are you even pregnant?"

"PREGNANT!" Chief Barclay retorts. "Brynn, you're pregnant?"

"Dad, leave it alone," she pleads.

"You're PREGNANT! For this fool?"

"WHOA! We don't know who the father is," Kage scoffs.

"Are you denying my daughter?"

"Look," Kage replies, "I don't know what kind of freak show stunt you two are trying to pull, but I'm DONE! Chief Barclay, thanks for the offer, but no thanks." Kage slams the door.

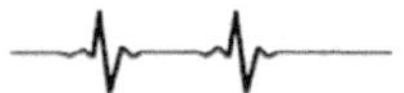

"Kage please, just hear me out," Brynn begs, standing outside of his vehicle.

"I just want to go," he counters.

"Please."

"Fine, get in."

Brynn enters the car. "I'm sorry."

"For what? What exactly are you sorry for?"

"All of it."

"You gotta do better than that. You have me looking like a fool. How many people knew that the Chief was your father?"

"It wasn't exactly a secret."

"Don't try that. You used me for something. Now tell me what it was."

"I haven't been stalking you, but your reputation does proceed you. And I don't just mean physically. My dad only wants the best workers for his hospital."

"So I've heard," he mumbles.

"I found out about you through my friend. The MC."

"Yeah, I remember her."

"She told me about a student who had the highest GPA in the Anesthesiology department and I looked you up. I didn't know it was you, my dance partner from Argentina. But, I thought, how perfect. It wouldn't have taken much convincing for you to join."

"Sounds like some kind of cult."

Brynn rolls her eyes. "Nothing like that. Our family just wants the best."

"What is your role in the hospital?" Kage asks.

"Public Relations Executive and Marketing Director."

"How befitting."

"Don't do that. You wanted me. I saw how you looked at me in Argentina. I didn't force you to do anything. So cut that out."

"You got what you wanted… I interned at the hospital, but babygirl, I will **NEVER** be a doctor at GSMH as long as the Barclays are in charge."

"Wow. You really are stupid. Passing up an opportunity of a lifetime because of a misunderstanding?"

"This wasn't a misunderstanding," Kage says. "You straight up **LIED** to me."

"Withheld information, there's a difference."

"Well BRA-VO for vocabulary Ms. Rizo-Barclay. Are you even pregnant?"

"How could you ask me such a thing?" she snaps. "You were there at my ultrasound appointment."

"I want a DNA test."

"You'll get your test," Brynn shrugs. "I have no doubt in my mind that you're the father."

"I need to think about this. Are you done with your confessions?"

Brynn exits the vehicle. "I am. No matter what happened between us, please note that I expect you to be at my beck and call regarding these pregnancy cravings. And to be in my child's life. OKAY! See you around Mr. Hunter."

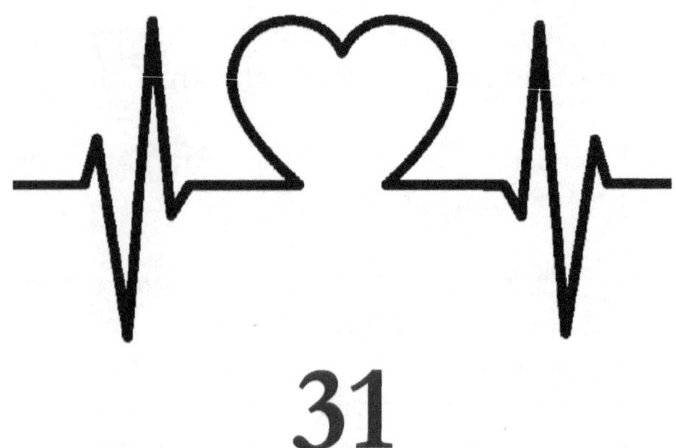

31

July

"I'm so over Brynn. This is torture…" Kage says, clicking off the phone. The constant barrage of calls annoyed his core.

"Kage? Kage? Is that you?"

He turns around in the direction of the voice. "Ember?"

She hugs him. "How long has it been?"

"I don't know."

"You look miserable," Ember chuckles. "What's been happening?"

"I don't have anything to say to you. You've ruined my life one too many times."

"Come on Kage, that's water under the bridge. So long ago. I've graduated. You're a senior now. I heard you're in the bridge program."

"News travels fast I see."

"I guess," Ember shrugs. "So where are you headed?"

"To the park for a run."

"Can I join?"

"I'd rather you not. My life's real complicated. I don't need any more drama with women."

"Me? Drama?" Ember squeals.

Kage shoots her a look. "Are you forge—"

Ember places a finger on his lips. "You know what your problem is? You talk too much. That's why you've gotten in so much trouble since you entered university. You gloat. You brag. JUST TALK TALK TALK! Shut up for once."

He grabs her wrist. "Don't TOUCH ME!"

"Ohhh, I miss your dominance, Mr. Hunter."

"This isn't a joke, Ember. I'm not a freshman."

She walks around him. "No, you are not," Ember flirts. "I see you've been working out in the right places."

Kage's face turns red.

Ember giggles. "I see that I still turn you on."

His phone rings. "I have to take this."

"Is that your mommy?" she mocks.

"Bye Ember," he says, walking away.

"See you around."

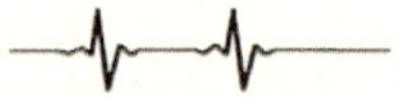

"What took you so long?" Brynn barks.

"Bumped into someone."

"Kage, I don't care, I'm hungry. Did you bring it?"

He hands her a tub of ice-cream.

Grabbing a spoon, Brynn begins to devour its contents.

"Save me some…" Kage chuckles.

Brynn growls at him. "LEAVE!"

"I'm really tired, can I hang around for a few minutes?"

"I SAID LEAVE! You're not needed anymore."

"Sheesh, you women and your hormones."

"EXCUSE ME?" she says, pushing him against the door.

"If you were not pregnant, we'd have gotten it on. I love feisty," Kage winks.

"We can still have sex while I'm pregnant."

Kage gags. "That doesn't appeal to me in the slightest."

"You don't think I'm sexy anymore?"

"Let's just leave it. I don't need to be punched right now. I'm going."

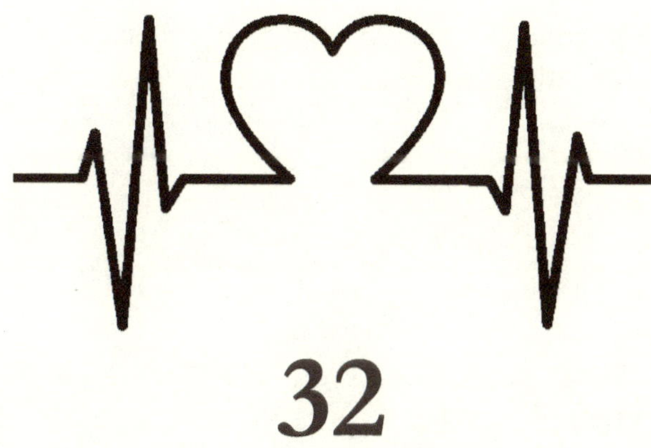

32

The Next Day

Kage walks to the water's edge and begins to skip rocks. "I can't believe I'm going to be a father. Me? The Hunter? In the prime of my life." He sighs.

"A lot on your mind?"

"Oh, hey Ember. Didn't notice anyone standing there."

"You are too young for a melancholy demeanor," she answers.

"Honestly, I have nothing to say to you."

She points to a nearby log. "Let's go sit. Catch up a little."

"Fine," he grumbles.

"I've never seen you like this. What's wrong?"

"Ember, what do you want?"

"Nothing. Can't I talk to an old friend?"

Kage rolls his eyes. "If it's one thing I've learned about you women, it's that you always **want something**."

"Have you looked in the mirror lately?"

"I don't hide my desire for the physical. But you women, hmmmm. I can't even count how many times I've been lied to."

"Sounds like you're having an emotional breakdown of sorts," Ember laughs.

"This isn't funny."

"I hate seeing you like this. What's really going on?"

Kage looks at Ember, sighing as he revealed his status. "She's pregnant."

"Who is?"

"This woman I met."

"How interesting," Ember replies. "What's so special about her?"

"Special has nothing to do with it. I'm not ready to be anyone's father. And to top it off, the baby's a girl."

Ember laughs out loud. "WOW! That's EPIC PAYBACK! I know how players are with their daughters."

"I'm glad you find this amusing…"

"Do you want to be with her? This woman?" she grimaces.

Kage shakes his head.

"Come on. Let's go."

"Where are we going?"

Ember grabs his hand. "You'll see when we get there…"

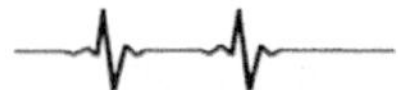

"Where are we?"

"This is my place. You can crash here for a few days if you like."

"Ember, I have a home. I'm good."

"You look like you need to unwind a bit," she says, pulling him close.

"What are you doing?" he snaps.

"Kage, I know that you still want me, even after all that's happened. I'm giving you the opportunity. No strings attached. You look like you haven't had any in a while."

He pushes her away.

"You don't want me?" Ember whimpers.

Kage has a moment of internal struggle. Scanning her body and noticing her curves, his mind goes back to Brynn. "I can't. I have enough problems with this baby on the way. I don't need any more pregnancy scares."

"We'll use protection. Double up," she offers.

"As much as I'd love to **unwind**—"

"Come on Kage, no strings attached."

"Sorry Ember. Maybe in another lifetime. But I'm off women for a while. Don't need a bunch of **Hunters** running around the place." His phone rings. "Hello?"

"Where are you?" Brynn yells into the receiver.

"I'm around."

"Do I hear a female in the background?"

"What are you talking about?"

"Kage, don't play with me," she snaps. "I hear a female in the background."

"No one's talking. You're hearing things."

"I. DIDN'T. SAY. TALKING. I can hear her breathing. Is she next to you? Does she know that I'm pregnant with your daughter? HOW DARE YOU CHEAT ON ME!"

"Brynn, please stop yelling. We're not even a couple."

"So you're admitting that there's a female near you?"

"Yes," he says nonchalantly. "Did you want something?"

"I have a doctor's appointment today. You need to be there."

"I'm about 2 hours away from you."

"The appointment is at 5:30. I **expect** to see you there!" She clicks off the phone.

Ember gives him a look.

"What?"

"I didn't expect that," she scoffs.

He stares at her blankly.

"That you'd end up with a crazy baby momma."

"First of all, the term *baby momma* is deplorable. Secondly, if that woman is pregnant, I know I'm not the father. Just waiting for a DNA test to prove it."

"You're sticking to that story?"

He nods. "Very much so. I used protection."

"Protection doesn't work 100%."

"Condoms aren't the only protection I have."

"Wow," Ember claps. "You got some next level protection? Please tell me what it is."

"Can't," Kage declines. "I've been sworn to secrecy."

"By who?"

"The person who made it. It hasn't been patented yet, but I've used it since I was about 16 and no scares… until now, so that's why I know she's lying."

"Whatever, you've always acted like you're above everything and everyone when it comes to rules. One fine day, you'll learn a lesson you'll never forget."

"Are you some kinda psychic now?" he laughs.

"Nope. I just know how life works."

"I know," Kage smiles. "Life… My ex-fling, who ruined my life twice, wants to get in my pants. Life is reeeeaaaallllyyyy interesting."

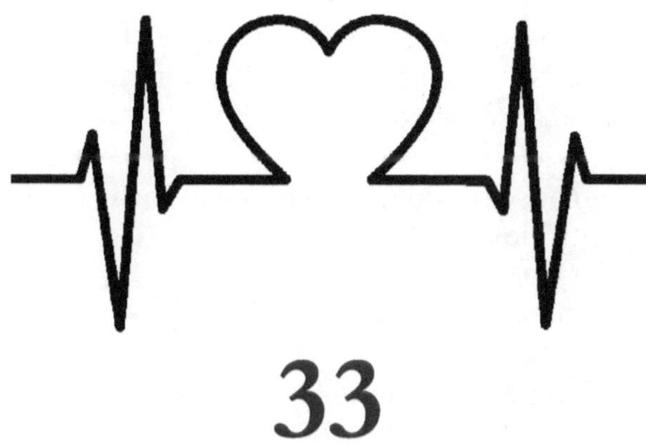

33

August
Aijikai, Kalanailani

Ember smiles as Kage hugged her from behind.

"Why'd you invite me on this trip?"

"I needed some time away from all that pregnancy drama. And I thought a plus one would be fine, you know for those moments…"

"Well, we do go way back," she giggles. "But you didn't need to rent a yacht."

"I missed being out on the water. It's been years. Not accustomed to life on the land. Hunters love the ocean."

"What else do Hunters love?" she says, kissing him.

"That… and other things…"

"I have a question. Please don't be mad."

"Ask away."

"What would happen if she really is pregnant and you **are** the father?"

Kage's forehead creases. "That would defy all types of scientific laws."

"But, it's not impossible."

"I really don't want to think about that while I'm on vacation. That's not why I invited you here."

"What exactly are we doing, Kage?"

"You tell me."

"I got a sexy man, we're floating on the waters, dancing to the rhythm of life. I'm just going with the flow. We don't need to define anything."

"Speaking of dancing," Kage says, "care to join me?"

"There's no music."

"Not that type of dancing," he winks.

"Oh, well alright now, let's do this…"

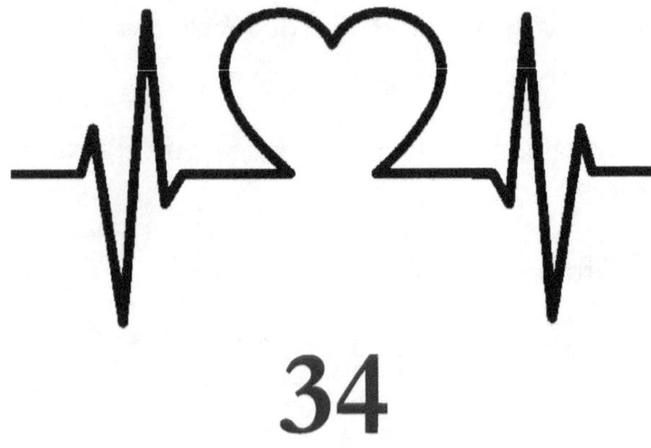

34

"Kalanailani is such a beautiful country. I can't believe this is my first time here," Ember says, later that night. "Did you hear what I said?"

Kage shrugs. "My mind is far. I'm sorry. Can we go walk on the beach?"

"Sure," she says, perplexed.

He takes her hand gently.

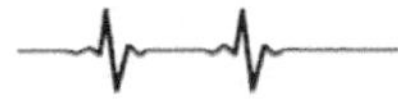

Kage sighs in contentment. "That's more like it."

"I really didn't think you'd want to be near the water after we spent the entire day on the yacht."

The air was suddenly filled with tango music.

"That's my song. Wanna dance?"

"I don't know how to tango," Ember declines.

"Come on, I'll show you."

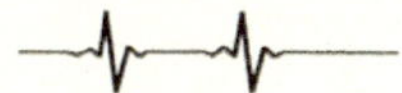

"Sorry, this is a masked party," the events coordinator announces, when they arrived at the entrance.

"We didn't bring any," Kage replies.

"Do you want to charge it to your room?" the woman asks.

"How much?"

"$35 each."

"Thirty-five dollars?" Kage scoffs. "What kinda masks are they?"

"Uniquely designed by the Master of Masquerade himself, *Sotos Belmonte.*"

"I don't care who designed it, that's expensive for something I'm only gonna use tonight."

"Kage, are we going in or not?" Ember whines. "It's getting chilly out here."

"Here," Kage grumbles as he handed the woman his credit card. "And I'd like a receipt."

"Thank you, enjoy the party," the woman smiles.

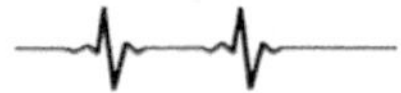

"Since when is money an object for you?"

"If I'm going to be a father, I can't live in luxury anymore. Children are expensive."

"Look at that, Mr. Kage Hunter is thinking about someone other than himself? He's ***adulting?*** Whattttt?" Ember stresses, sarcastically. "Never thought I'd see the day. You better do grown up stuff."

"Cut the sarcasm," he laughs, leading her to the dance floor.

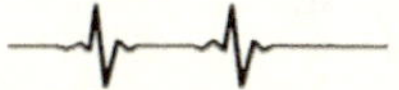

"I know those moves anywhere," Kage says as he watched the man and woman dance in precision.

"Will you pay attention? You're supposed to be teaching me the tango," Ember grimaces, as he stepped on her foot.

"Give me a second."

"Kage, where are you going?" she calls out.

"I'm sorry, can I cut in?"

The male dancer looks at Kage, shrugs, and walks away.

"So, you followed me here?" Kage asks the woman. "Oh, you have nothing to say? Your stomach feels mighty flat for a woman who is supposed to be pregnant—"

"EXCUSE ME!" the woman yells. "PREGNANT? I don't even know you."

"Oh, my bad, I'm sorry miss. I thought you were someone else."

She removes the mask from her face.

"Wrong person," Kage chuckles. "You should go find your dance partner."

Ember runs over to them. "You left me to go dance with her?"

"Sorry, those moves, the tantalizing way she moved… Reminds me of someone."

"Great. I'm competing with a figment of your imagination."

Ember hands Kage an ice pack. He grimaces as the coldness hit his cheek.

"You deserved that," she chuckles.

"I didn't expect that woman to come back and slap me so hard. I apologized."

"Stop talking."

Kage tosses the ice pack in the sink. "I really do need to take a break from women. All this suffering isn't good for my well-being."

Ember stares at him.

"Say what you need to."

"I'm at a loss for words, Mr. Hunter."

His phone vibrates.

"You can answer it." Ember rolls her eyes.

"One thing I don't need from you is your permission," he says, getting up.

Kage looked at the notification on his phone…

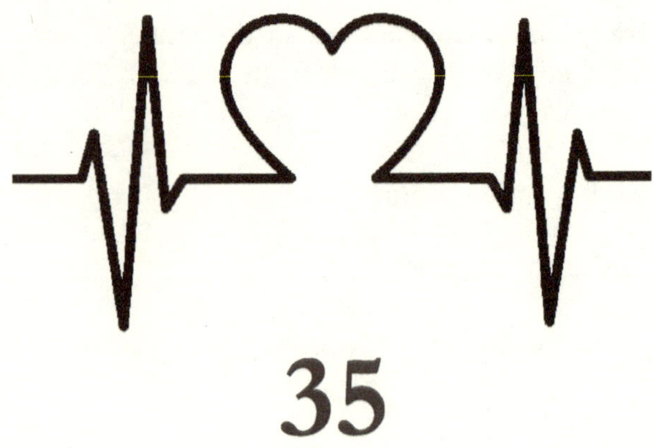

35

Ember Kighland
&
Fox Stoneshire II
ARE ENGAGED
Official wedding details on page 8.

"What's the meaning of this?" Kage snapped.

"I don't even know what you're looking at," Ember shrugged.

"This tabloid... it says you're engaged."

Ember laughs.

"You're engaged?"

"I am. What's the big deal? I thought we were having fun?" She grabs on to his arm.

"Get off me," he snaps. "You see, this is why I don't trust women. You all **LIE**."

"You should be the last one to talk about lies, Kage. THE VERY LAST ONE!"

"No, you're not going to play victim here. What do you get out of this? Aren't you tired?"

She continues to laugh. "You're not the only one who can be a player. I needed to know that I was still capable of having any man I wanted."

"You're sick. Something is seriously wrong with you."

"No Mr. Hunter, **YOU** are the sick one. I'm just one of your *symptoms.*"

"Get out of my face. I'm done with you. No need to explain further. You've gotten what you wanted from me. Public humiliation, extortion, and now wasted time. Bravo, Ember, bravo."

Her laughter continues, as she closes in his door.

I'm done with women. Seriously… This can't be all there is to life.

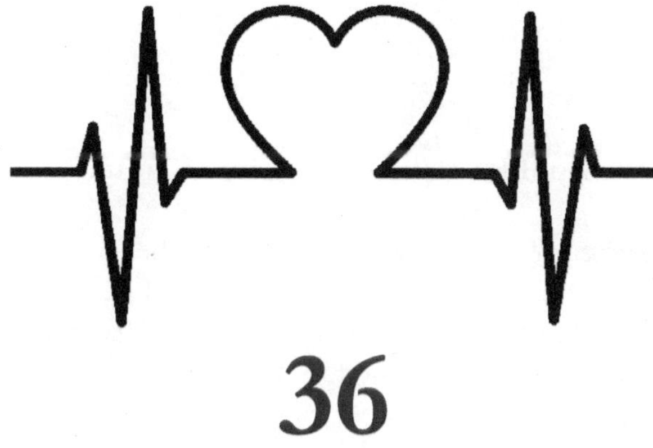

36

Months Later

Kage took a swig of his drink, tosses the can on the sand, and jumps into the water.

"Vermont, Vermont," a boy yells, "I think that man is drowning."

Without a second thought, the man dives into the water and pulls a motionless Kage on to the sand. "Come on buddy, wake up, wake up." He performs CPR. No response. Vermont looks up to the sky, "God please, spare his life…"

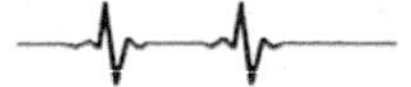

Boulder Lake University Hospital

Vermont Sözne went down to the beach for a baptism. As the youth pastor, he'd seen his fair share of troubled souls, but something about this man seemed familiar.

"How is he, doctor?"

"We were able to remove the water from his lungs. He's going to live. That was a miracle if I'd seen one. This man should've been dead," the doctor replies.

"Thanks sir."

"Is he your brother?"

"No, I was just in the right place at the right time," Vermont answers.

"Lucky him."

"Not luck. God saved him."

"Well, whoever this god is, that young man needs to thank them for the rest of his life." He pauses. "If you'll excuse me…"

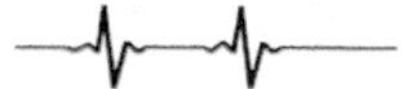

A week had passed since Kage had been in the hospital. He couldn't remember the event that led him there.

"You have a visitor," his nurse announces.

"I do?" Kage looks into the doorway. A man stood there with a pleasant smile on his face.

"I'll leave you to it," the nurse says, closing the door.

"Are you the one who saved me?" Kage asks.

"No, I'm just a vessel," Vermont replies.

"You don't look like a ship to me," he chuckles, through the pain.

"Relax son."

"Were you there when it happened?"

Vermont nods.

"I can't remember that day."

"Do you remember anything?" Vermont asks.

"Of course, my name is Kage Hunter. I am a 22-year-old med student, but I took a break from school because a woman lied to me about being pregnant with my child. And I swore off women. All they do is lie. And I'm done chasing skirts, pants, or whatever they have on."

"Seems like you've reached a crossroad?"

"I guess," Kage shrugs.

"I'm happy that your memory is intact."

"Except that part. Doctor said I almost drowned. Is that true?"

"Yes, I was at the beach to conduct a baptism service when one of the youths called out that you were drowning and I just dove into the water. God definitely had me there for a purpose."

"God? Baptism? What is all that? I don't believe in God."

"God loves you more than anyone ever will. And that day, HE chose for me to be there just so your life can be spared. John 3:16, *'For*

God so loved the world that he gave his one and only Son, that whoever believes in him shall not perish but have eternal life."

"So this God sent his son to die so that I wouldn't?"

"That's correct," Vermont replies.

Kage laughs. "You can't possibly believe that…"

"I do and I've experienced HIS love for myself."

"No one loves without expecting something in return. Allowing your child to die so others can live? That doesn't make sense."

"God isn't like man. HE is the definition of love. And because of HIS love, HE sent HIS son. It doesn't have to make sense for it to be true. As a medical student you would've come across theories that isn't logical, but based on your **practical** experience, it resonated with you."

"I don't see the correlation," Kage replies.

"You have to believe to see. Choose to believe. It doesn't work any other way.

Because it's not something that can be explained," Vermont adds.

"You're saying that in order for me to **see** I have to believe first? Doesn't that go against the saying, *seeing is believing*?"

"Christians don't view things like the unsaved man. We believe and therefore we see."

"Man, get outta here with that crazy talk. I don't want your Christianity, god, beliefs, or strange love."

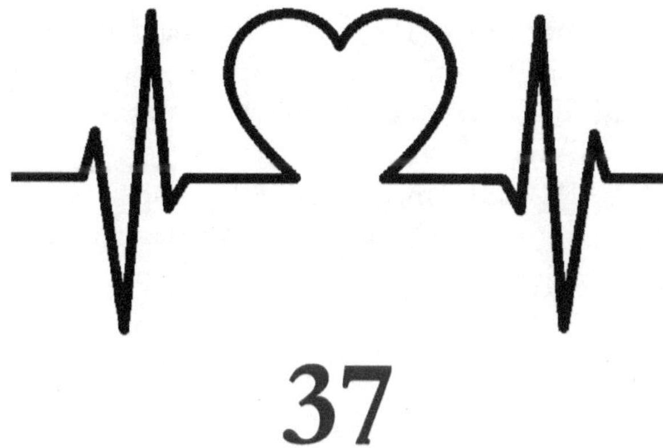

37

"I can't believe it's been eight years since I've been sharing my escaping death testimony," Kage smiles.

"And I can't believe you're Dr. Hunter," Vermont chuckles.

"Whatever man. I'm just happy to have met such a great friend."

"Don't get all mushy on me, man."

"What should I talk about?"

"Move as the Lord leads. I know that you've struggled to share your **full** testimony, but I hope that one day you will."

"I'm not ready. This has been a hard journey for me. I'm thirty now and so much has changed. I don't want to relive my past."

"As I said, move as HE leads. Your testimony isn't about you. I know that one day you'll share it."

"If you say so."

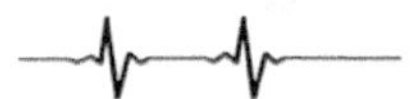

Kage scanned the crowd. His nerves grew as it finally dawned on him the amount of people that sat in the audience. 45,000 people sat with bated breath as he tried to formulate his response. It was Q&A time at the conference. Everything seemed to be going well until the young woman came to the podium and asked, *"Why are all men players?"*

Although she didn't look much younger than him, he looked at her as though she was a little girl. Remorse filled his heart as the word ***player*** rang in the atmosphere.

In that moment, he remembered Marwa's words from years ago, "*I hope some woman breaks your heart the way you've broken so many of our hearts. Better yet, I hope you* **die ALONE**

AND MISERABLE! *You're nothing but a* **low** ***self-esteem LOSER!'***

No amount of prayer, fasting, repentance, or preaching could've erased all the guilt Kage had for the number of women's lives he'd ruined. Although he accepted God's forgiveness, he couldn't find it in his heart to forgive himself. He wondered if this was what the Apostle Paul meant when he spoke about the *thorn in his flesh.*

Vermont taps Kage' shoulder, snapping him out of his thoughts. "You okay, man?"

"I'm good. Just trying to formulate my words."

"Let God lead," Vermont counters.

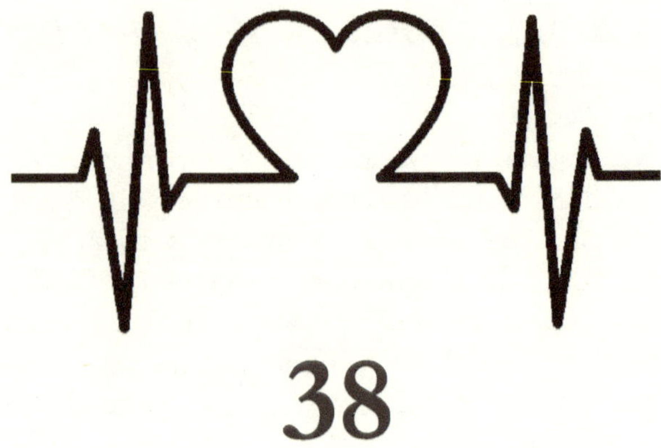

38

"Thank you so much for being brave and asking that question. But I'd like to make a correction, all men *are NOT players.* The world has just **highlighted** them to a magnitude that we think is the general consensus. I assure you that good, godly, regenerated men exist. You'll hear many women's testimony of their husbands being faithful. I'm not denouncing your question or possible experience, but I just wanted to put that out there before it traveled too far in the environs. ***All men are NOT players!***

What I'm about to share with you is my truth. I was given many names, and player was top of the list. But there was a genesis to that behavior…

When I was twelve, I accidentally walked in to an art show featuring nude models. Instead of being kicked out, the gallery owner opened my appetite…

My parents invited me to a private interactive demonstration. One of their friends, a local Anesthesiologist, was going to showcase one of his groundbreaking discoveries. I was so excited because children aren't allowed behind the scenes in the medical world. I ended up going through the wrong door. But what I heard, caught my attention…

'…It's a man's job to enjoy a woman's body. Each body is unique. And you'd only know what you like after you've had sex with her. The eyes can only see so much, but when you've experienced her fullness, it's like nothing you've known.'

The gallery owner saw me peeking and instead of chasing me away, she called me in. All the women just stood there.

I went up to the owner and bravely asked, *'Aren't I too young for sex?'*

'Shhhh,' she replied. 'Listen to your heart. See how it's racing? That's how you'd know what's worth the conquest. But don't do anything until you're 16. You'll be legal then.'

'Why are you telling me this?'

'I believe in repopulating the earth. Anytime I come across a young man such as yourself, I make it my duty to school him on the bodily arts. My man loves my body, but I allow him to explore others. All for art of course. And I too, dabble from time to time with the male specimens I see.'

'I don't get it.'

'What's your name?' she asked.

'Kage Hunter.'

'It's okay young Hunter. What a nice name. It'll take you places. Remember, you're the hunter and every woman **you want** *is your prey… When you taste you'll understand.'*

'Taste what?'

'That's it. You've seen enough…"

Kage looked into the audience and then at Vermont, who encouraged him to continue.

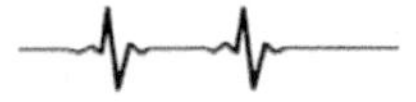

The dark clouds of Kage' past shrouded the atmosphere… He sighed as his mind went back to the places he'd long blocked out…

"After that experience I started watching pornography on the computer and watched every Rated XXX movie that ever existed. It's illegal and blocked in Starr Islands, so whenever we went on vacation or abroad for my parents' work, I'd look at them. They never knew what I saw that day or what I was doing. By the time I had my first sexcapade at 16, I was a goner. She told me I was her only one and I believed her, until I saw her boyfriend picking her up after school one day. College girl around 21. She lied to me. That's **all** women do.

And after that I vowed to conquer as many women on and off campus as I can until I was done. I didn't know how much it affected me. I've hurt so many women for years. The crazy part is when they hurt me, I didn't care, it just fueled my mantra: ALL WOMEN LIE. The lady at the gallery and every single woman who duped me in some way or form… LIARS!

Blaming them was pointless. I made all the bad choices in my life. I don't know why I didn't tell my parents about that first experience at the nude show. I mean, why would they even have a show like that in the same building with medical professionals.

I never judged anyone's conquests and I still don't. Some of you sitting will probably be labeled by this young lady as a *player*. But I learned that's not all there is to life." He laughs out loud. "You know, funny thing? I remember something that my college roommate said to me, *'Sex isn't all there is to life…One day you're going to look back and regret that list you have.'* I can honestly say that he was right. Sex isn't all there is to life and I have lived in regret.

I haven't thought much about marriage, but I can't imagine marrying a woman and she found out about my hideous past. To know that she wasn't my first and only. God is still working on me in that department. Thinking that I'm not good enough to be with a special woman one day. It pains me to think that there may be other women laughing at her because of me.

I don't have it all together and I won't pretend that I do. One thing I know is God loves me. HE doesn't see me as a loser, nasty player, but a broken man in need of HIM, daily. I can't live life without HIM.

So that's a summarized version of my story and you're the first people to hear it. I'm not sure who it's meant for, but God loves you. None of us are perfect. None of us can judge anyone. Only the Father and HE chose to send HIS son instead, so that we don't die without knowing HIM.

If I died on the day I almost drowned, I don't want to think of where I would've ended up. Every day is a gift. Every day that you breathe is God's gift to you. What you do with that gift determines where you spend eternity: heaven or hell. There's no alternative. Only two options, and it's up to you to choose which one. No one is going to force you to choose. And not choosing is also a choice. There's no repentance, forgiveness, tears, drama, or buyouts in heaven. The choice is yours and the choice is **NOW**!

I'm not going to lie and say that once you accept Jesus Christ as your Lord and Savior that your life will be peachy. I'm also not encouraging you to choose Jesus *just to avoid going to hell.* What I'm saying is, choose eternity from now. While you're still in the land of the living. No matter how cliché it sounds, tomorrow isn't promised to anyone…"

When Kage finished his testimony, the audience erupted in applause.

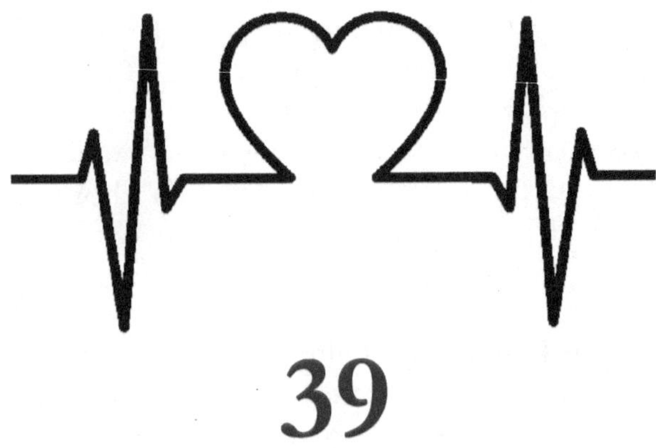

39

"Have a seat, Kage,"' Vermont requests.

"Oh boy, every time I heard that in the past, I was in some kind of trouble."

"Nothing like that."

"Alrighty, let's hear it. How'd I do?"

Vermont looks at him. "This isn't about a grade. You shared your testimony. And you impacted a lot of it. I just got off the phone with another one of the counselors. Altogether 400 young men turned in their player's cards because of your testimony. Another 1,500 rededicated their lives to Christ. And 21,008 people gave their hearts to Christ. People traveled from far to this conference to hear about the one who almost drowned, but lived to tell the story. Big news in Starr Islands. Not knowing that woman would be brave enough to ask a true player about players. I'm sorry, *former player*. Gotta make sure to denounce that."

"Amen," Kage agrees. "That's amazing news."

"You've been invited to share your testimony at the **UpRising Conference** in California next year."

"California? I haven't been to the US before. I heard there's been a drastic change in the spiritual climate over the past few years. People are getting saved and sharing the gospel. Even the media's narrative has changed. Prayer really works."

"Yes, and we will continue to pray for them," Vermont replies.

"How does discipleship work in these large crowds? Because it's one thing to be saved, but the follow up is where many congregations fall short."

"Our congregation belongs to a global discipleship ministry, where we continuously teach and encourage people to not only share the gospel, but mentor new believers in the faith. We emphasize that discipleship is about time. Building relationships with people, connecting with their humanity and showing them the spiritual connection."

"First time I'm hearing about it."

"It was an initiative started at last year's UpRising Conference. Many of the leaders shared their concern about the follow up aspect in the lives of new believers. With all that's going on in the world and people falling away from the faith, it's hard to decipher the true leaders from the false. Without discernment it's difficult to *test the spirits*, but God has been changing the guards and raising up men, women, boys, and girls to share HIS truth. The only truth that matters."

"I'm so thankful to be part of the body of Christ. We're not perfect, but together, with God's leading we can do so much for the Kingdom. Sharing our testimonies, writing books, and just fulfilling purpose, many will come to know Christ. And I'm happy that a former player like me, could be used to point people to Jesus because honestly without HIM our life is meaningless."

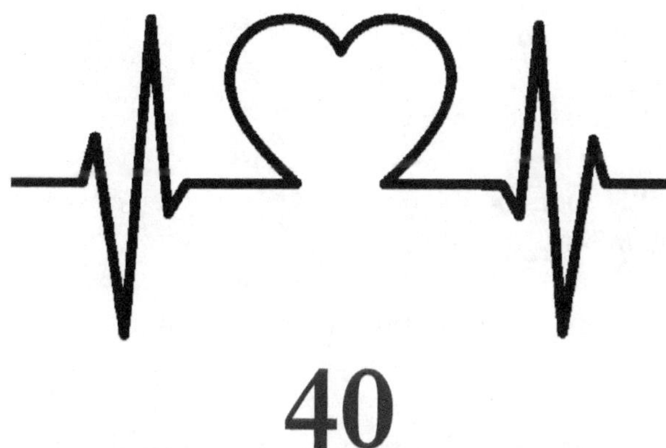

40

UpRising Conference
California, USA

"This place is packed. There must be at least 200,000 people in attendance," Kage says, as walked through the venue for the opening ceremony.

Vermont nods. "I gotta take this. My wife is calling."

"Don't have to tell me twice," Kage chuckles.

Moments later, Vermont returns. "Her flight is delayed until tomorrow. The storm's brewing in Grand Sierra Isla."

"We'll continue to pray."

"I miss her so much."

"Hopefully I'll be able to say that about a woman someday."

"Man please, your wife is definitely out there."

"Think so? I don't really think about it much, but watching you and Belle-Amore over the years has been inspiring."

"She's out there. And she will be perfect for you."

"Well," Kage laughs, "whoever she is I love her already."

The following morning, Kage headed to the breakfast area. Vermont went to the airport to pick up his wife and her friend.

I'm a big boy. He chuckled to himself. Finding an empty table in a nearby corner, he goes to sit down. "I haven't been by myself in over a decade. Loneliness…"

As he sat to eat lunch, Nouvel's name came to mind.

Nouvel? Why am I thinking about her?

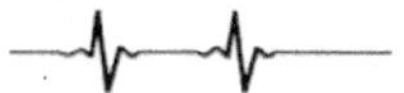

After lunch, Kage threw his garbage away and headed to the bathroom to wash his hands. He walked up the stairs to the speakers' lounge, when suddenly he bumps into a woman. "I'm so sorry, miss. My apologies. Can I help you pick those up?"

As the woman stood up, Kage gulped. She was definitely a beauty.

"That's okay, I got it, thanks."

"Kage, I want to introduce you to someone," Vermont announces. "This is my wife's friend. She's hosting one of the sessions later."

The woman from the staircase smiles up at him.

"Nice to meet you, miss—"

"Nouvel de Amico," the woman finishes.

Before Kage could pick up his jaw, the conference host calls them to the stage.

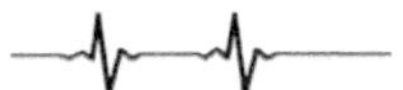

Although Kage was eager to share his story, he couldn't stop thinking about Nouvel as the words came out of his mouth. What was she doing in California?

"We'll see you back here in 90 minutes as we break for lunch," the host announces.

Kage scanned the room for Nouvel, but couldn't find her anywhere. Dejected, he made his way to the lunch area.

I gotta find her….

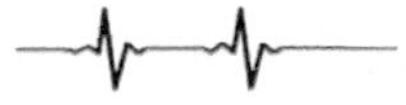

"Mind if I sit down?"

His heart leapt when he saw her. "Sure," he says, trying to play it cool. She didn't seem to recognize him.

"Nouvel, right?"

She nods. "I didn't catch your name."

"Uhhh—"

"Are you okay?" she asks.

Kage wasn't sure what Nouvel remembered about him. "Kage Hunter," he whispers.

"Ah, sorry, didn't quite get that," Nouvel giggles.

"Kage Hunter," he repeats, at his regular decibel.

Nouvel gags on her drink.

"Whoa, are you okay?" Kage asks, getting up out of his chair to help her.

"I'm fine," she bats him away. "Did you go to GSIU in Starr Islands?"

"I did."

"Did you ever have a roommate named Xerses?"

He nods.

"Wow, Kage Hunter. I'm sorry I didn't recognize you; you look so different."

"Is that a good or bad thing?"

"Good, definitely good," Nouvel says, hoping he didn't recognize her blushing.

Out of all the women he'd slept with, Nouvel hadn't made it to his conquest list. Guilt permeated his being as he thought of all the women who did.

"This is wow… So how have you been? What have you been up to?"

"I don't think we have enough time to talk about that right now."

"Oh, believe me, I'll make time. Maybe we can meet up after they close off tonight? I'm sure Belle-Amore won't mind if I miss our post-session hang out."

"Sounds good," he replies, trying not to sound too excited.

Nouvel looks so beautiful. I hope I don't say anything dumb to mess things up later...

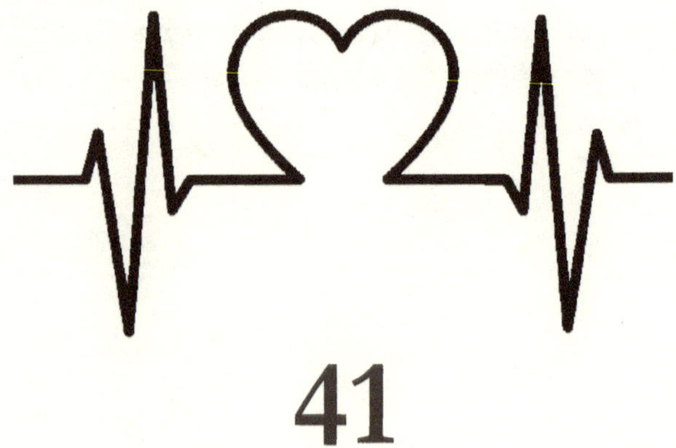

41

"Kage, can I speak to you please?" Belle-Amore asks.

"Sure, did you need help with something?"

"Let's talk on the balcony."

He walks with her and they sit on the bench.

"I see you've been spending a lot of time with Nouvel for the past few days. Vermont and I love you like a brother. And Nouvel is like my baby sis. I understand that you two went to university together. What are your intentions?"

"I'm happy that she has someone who cares about her so much. Honestly, I don't know where I stand with her regarding a relationship. Still trying to figure out what's happening between us, actually."

"She's been through a lot and I don't want her to get hurt," Belle-Amore replies. "If you know that you're not ready for marriage, then I'd advise you to end it because she is ready for the next step."

"I understand. As I said, I'm still trying to figure things out. But thanks for this. It really means a lot to me."

"No problem," she smiles. "Now let's go back inside."

Kage grabs a drink from the fridge. "Want one?"

Nouvel declines. "What were you two talking about so secretively?"

"All you need to know is that Belle-Amore cares a lot about you. That's a great friend to have."

Nouvel gives him the side eye. "Okay Kage, whatever you say."

"Why is everyone looking so serious?" Vermont chuckles. "I thought we were here for game night?"

"Come on Kage, let's show them how it's done," Belle-Amore claps.

"Not a chance," Vermont laughs at his wife. "Nouvel and I got this."

"I had a great time, but I'm tired," Nouvel yawns.

"I can walk you to your room," Kage volunteers.

"It's only down the hall," Nouvel giggles.

"Let's go and leave the lovebirds for their nightcap." He waves to Vermont and his wife, as he exits with Nouvel.

"Why were you so hard on him?" Vermont asks, when they leave.

"Kage is a good guy. I've seen him grown leaps and bounds in the Lord. And I can say the same thing for Nouvel, but I'm worried."

"About what?"

"I know my girl and I can see that she likes him."

"What's wrong with that?" Vermont shrugs. "They look good together."

"But can they handle one another's past?"

"That's not for us to decide. Let God do HIS connecting. If they are meant to be, then it'll happen. God knows the purpose for which HE puts two people together."

"Yes, I know honey. I just wanna make sure that—"

"Shhh," he says, putting a finger to her lips, "enough about them, and let's take Bro. Hunter's advice and have that nightcap."

"Oh behave, Mr. Sözne," she blushes.

"I love it when you call me *mister*," he winks.

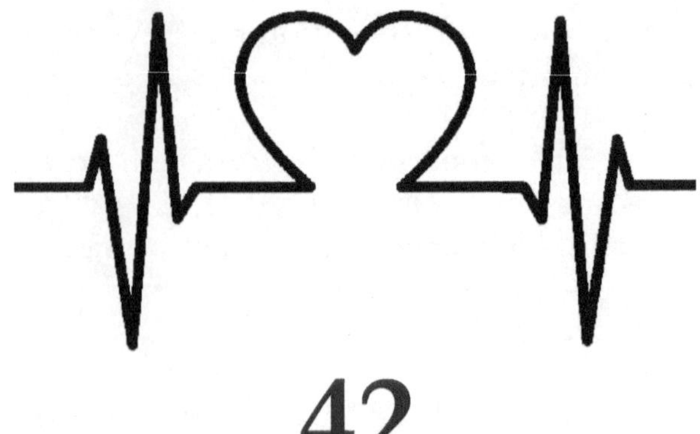

42

"Well, this is me," Nouvel announces.

"Good night," he says, shaking her hand.

She giggles. "So formal."

"I'll see you tomorrow."

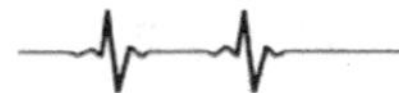

That night, neither Kage or Nouvel slept well. Something was definitely happening and they both needed answers…

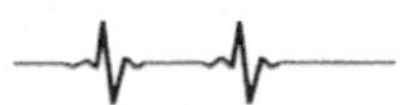

The next morning, Kage meets Nouvel for breakfast. It was day five of the weeklong conference.

"How'd you sleep?" Kage asks Nouvel, as they ate breakfast.

"I'd be able to answer that if I got **actual** sleep."

"Did something happen?"

"I don't know," she shrugs.

"I guess we're in the same boat. I didn't get much sleep either."

"There you two are," Vermont says. "We're about to start."

"We're coming," Nouvel replies. She turns her gaze back to Kage, "Can we talk tonight? I'd say lunchtime, but I'm heading out after this morning's session."

"Sure. See you later."

"Let's go," she says, taking his hand. "You're so extra."

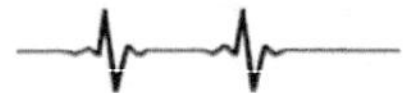

Throughout the day Kage couldn't stop thinking about Nouvel's request. In the past he had no problem talking to a woman, but everything with Nouvel was different. The way she carried about herself. She was as close to perfection as any woman could ever be. He often wondered how anyone like her would ever give a man like him a chance…

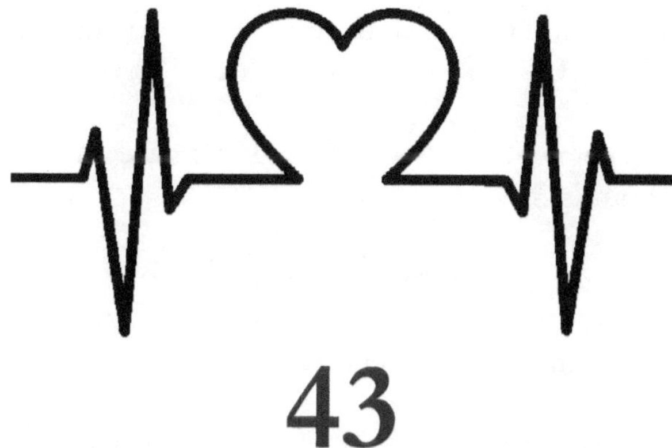

43

Around 8PM Kage met Nouvel in the conference ballroom, while some people mingled near the stage.

"You look beautiful," he says.

She blushes.

"What did you want to talk about?"

"We've been reconnecting since I arrived. And I want to clear the air. I'm not sure what's going on between us, but before we go any further friendship or otherwise, I need to share something with you."

Kage stares at her nervously.

Ten minutes passed and the silence still lingered. Tears began to fill Nouvel's eyes.

He gives her a tissue. "We don't have to talk about it."

"No, I feel comfortable enough to tell you. Whatever you choose to do with the information is your choice."

The reassuring smile on his face was a source of encouragement for her. She wiped her tears as she began to tell her story.

"I used to be ashamed to tell my story, but there's something about true deliverance. The number of men I've been with would make some church mothers **clutch their pearls.**

It all started when I was 15. I auditioned for a local movie as an extra and got the part. I met a man who said that he'd show me the ropes. What I didn't know was that he was a pimp. Sounds cliché, but that's my life. I didn't start having sex right away. He told me when I was 16 (aka legal adulthood in Starr Islands) that I should give him a call.

He connected me to one of his many women. Her name was 'Madam' and she mentored me. All behind the scenes. I wasn't allowed to tell anyone. Coming from a sheltered family I **wanted** to be rebellious, so I kept it a secret.

I met Rayce when I started university. I was told to have a boyfriend to keep up appearances. But every few weeks, when there was a break from classes or a long weekend, they'd fly me out to connect with high profile men from every continent. Yes, even Antarctica. The word '**arctic**' doesn't even begin to describe that place.

Anyways, no one knew. I just told people that I was going on auditions out of town. The men loved my 'smarts', so they'd buy me things to help with school.

I lost my scholarship very early in my freshman year. Never told my family. My 'main guy' sponsored me. He sent money to cover all my bills; school fees and rent included.

It was going well UNTIL the night before my wedding to Rayce. Apparently, one of the guys that I'd been with was his cousin. He tried to have sex with me that night. And when I said no, he told Rayce about our time together. The obscenities that came out of his mouth still rings in my ears.

The irony in all of this was that Rayce cheated on me for our entire relationship. *'You don't say no to a* ***Forrey...'*** I never said anything because I knew what I was doing. Honestly didn't expect him to find out. And I know what you're thinking... Yes, I WAS going to continue playing the field after I got married. I was in so deep.

Years later, I'm an actress, alone in the world, STILL giving myself to the highest bidder... Remorse wasn't part of my vocabulary. I just told myself, *'I'm an actress and THIS is my part.'*

The gigs became less and less. My manager said that the studios thought I was **washed up**. Me, Nouvel, washed up at 25? I felt low. Depressed. Suicidal.

And then, one day I went to a restaurant and cried as I ate. A lady came to me and just spoke into my life. I didn't know who she was at the time. Then I found out that she was none other than Tahira Mikos, not sure if you've heard of Tavario Mikos—"

"Of course, he's a famous movie star," Kage chimes in.

"Ex. He made that very clear when he left the acting circuit years ago. So yeah, I shared my life with her. She didn't judge me and connected me with her best friend, Kaiora, who had a similar lifestyle before her conversion. We talk almost every day. Both Tahira and Kaiora has invested so much in my life. I was invited to church, but it took me months to even step foot in the building.

Finally, after deciding there's nothing to lose, I went to a church service. I gave my heart to Jesus Christ and got baptized two months later. It's been about five years in my faith journey. I never thought that I'd still be able to pursue my passion. But I realized that God gave me that gift. I just needed to use it for HIM.

Tavario is still friends with people in the industry and got me connected to the acting group I'm with. They film and produce biblically based movies. And that's what I've been doing since…"

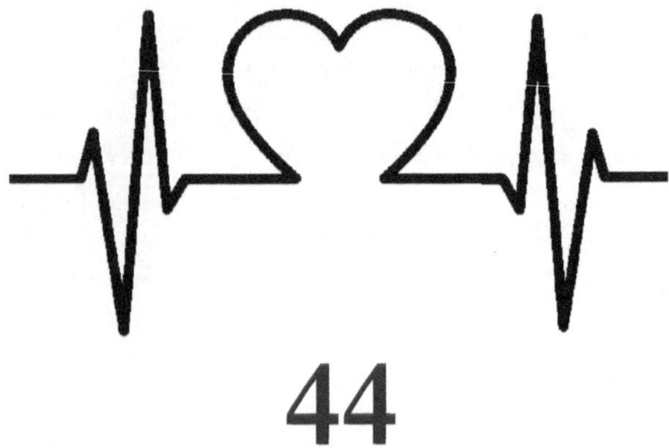

44

Moments passed between the two as Kage took in all that Nouvel divulged. Of course, he was in no position to judge anyone, but he was quite surprised that Nouvel wasn't as innocent as he'd previously thought. He was low key relieved.

"I know you'd probably not want to be with a woman with such a tainted past, but I just wanted to be honest with you. I guess I was the true player for real…"

"Nouvel, look at me," Kage says. "Is it okay if I hold your hands?"

She allows him to take her hands.

"I'm happy you shared that with me."

"You want to run for the hills, right? I know men want to marry virgins. And I'm far from one."

"I've never judged anyone and I don't intend on doing that now. I don't think any less of you. Actually, I won't lie, I'm relieved," he chuckles.

"Relieved how?"

"Well, you know my past and I was no saint. I always wondered what it would be like to disclose such secrets to my woman, whoever she is. But there's an undeniable connection between us. I say we form a friendship and see what happens. I'm in no rush for any exclusivity. Truth be told, I loved you ever since we meet. I just didn't know it."

"Me?" Nouvel blushes. "Why me?"

"I remember when you came to greet your brother on dorm and I saw you… I said WHOA that's a beauty right there."

"Oh stop."

"I'm serious. A few of my exes asked me if I liked you, but I denied it because I didn't know how I felt. However, you were there in my heart behind all the foolishness."

"Why does it seem like that's the sweetest thing you've ever said in your life?"

Kage laughs. "Y'all women know how to turn a man, don't you? I'm still a Hunter, so I'll pursue you properly. You're not gonna get the Hunter just like that," he winks.

Nouvel rolls her eyes. "I see your sense of humor is still there."

"It never left. All that mushiness was making me queasy," he snickers. "In all seriousness though, I want to pursue you the right way. First, have a conversation with dear old Mr. de Amico, your father…"

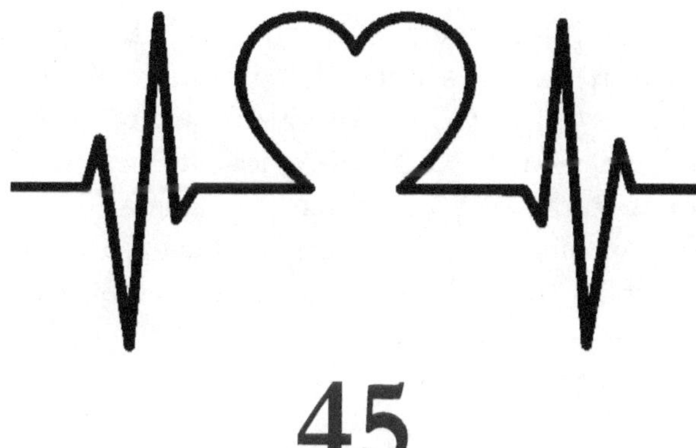

45

Later that night, Nouvel made her way to Belle-Amore's room. She knocked on the door, "Can I come in?"

"Sure, Vermont's downstairs in a meeting. I know you talked to him. Tell me everything."

"I told him my truth," Nouvel reveals.

"And what did he say?"

"It was the weirdest response. The man said he's relieved."

"Relieved?" Belle-Amore asks, perplexed.

Nouvel nods. "He said that he's happy that he didn't have to explain his past to me."

"You both have a story, so there's that. But to hear that he's not judging you, hmmmm, that's really God. Although you're both Christians now, I know a lot of men who **expect** their wives to have a squeaky-clean background. No skeletons… baggage… or anything. Just Ms. Perfect. Kage sees beyond that. The way that man looks at you, girl, I'm telling you he's hooked."

"We haven't made anything official yet, but he did say he wants to talk to my father."

"Well, alrighty then. That's a great start. No games. This man knows what he wants."

"I'd say so," Nouvel squeals. "I don't mean to jump ahead, but this may be it." She fans herself. "Kage could be the one, my one. I never thought in a million years that I'd like **Kage Hunter**, but I do."

"Did you have feelings for him back then?"

Nouvel shakes her head. "Nope, I just saw him as *the freshman* and my brother's **well-known roommate**. That's it. Wait til Xerses hears this…"

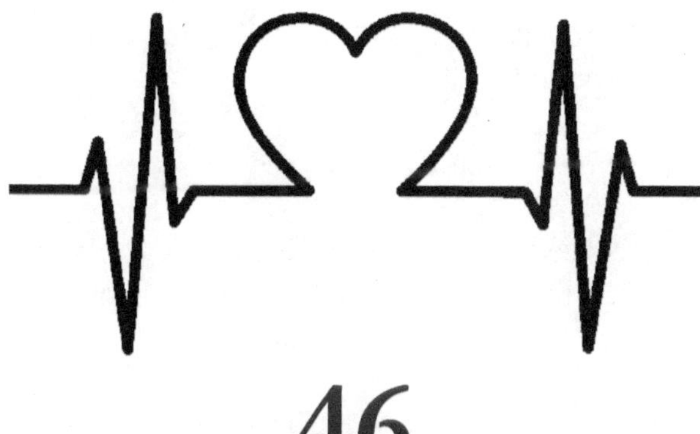

46

When they arrived back in Grand Sierra Isla, Kage had a hard decision to make. The request from the Lord was difficult, but he knew that it would benefit him in the long run.

They sat in his car. "Nouvel, I have to tell you something," Kage says, breaking the silence.

She looks at him with innocent eyes.

"Um," he clears his throat. "We have to put a pin in our relationship."

Nouvel tried to hold back the tears. "Is something wrong? Did you change your mind about me?"

"It's not like that. During the plane ride, the Lord spoke to me about us."

She sighs. "What did HE say?"

"We need to take a month's break from one another to hear from HIM clearly on how to proceed with our relationship."

No words came out of her mouth.

"I know," Kage exhales. "I don't understand it, but I have to be obedient. I've spent the past few years learning to hear God's voice and HE was **extremely** vocal on the plane."

"What are the stipulations for this time apart?"

"No contact whatsoever and no seeing one another. We have to tell Vermont and Belle-Amore. They are to walk with us through the process. We cannot ask them anything about one another, but we can confide in them if something arises. We can agree on a time to come together and discuss whatever the Lord has laid on our hearts regarding our future, whether it's to be together..." he pauses, "or not."

"Okay, well, there's nothing that I can do, so... When do we start?"

"As soon as you exit this vehicle," he says trying not to cry.

"Bye for now, Kage," Nouvel kisses his cheek.

Now why did she have to do that?

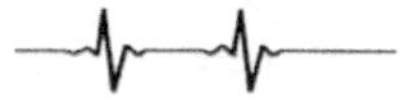

Nouvel dialed Belle-Amore's number.

"Are you okay?"

"Girl, I don't know if I can do this. I miss Kage so much."

"Nouvel, it's only been one day."

"I know," she whimpers. "I feel like that time during fasting when you have to give up on food… All the time you can go without eating for days, but as soon as you say the word **fast**, here comes your stomach making all kinds of whale noises. That's how I'm feeling now."

"I'm here for you, so message me, call me whenever you need to. And I know you have Tahira and Kaiora to help as well. Just don't ask me **anything** about Mr. Hunter. I'm going to abide by the rules. This is hard for me too…"

"How so?"

"Well, I have to force myself NOT to ask Vermont about his conversations with Kage," Belle-Amore chuckles. "That's hard, cuz I wanna know if he's missing you too."

"You're so extra. It's probably for the best. It's going to be a hard month, but I need to focus on Jesus and see what HE wants for my future, with or without Kage," she sighs.

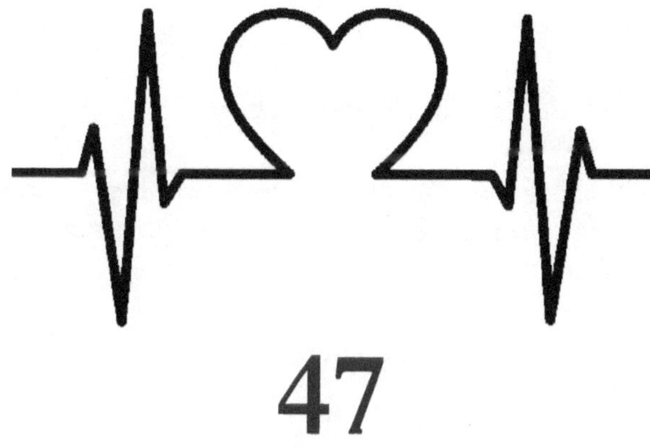

47

Two Weeks Later

"Doctor Hunter, the patient's wife has a question about the procedure."

"Sure, send her in," Kage replies to the nurse.

Moments later, Ember stood at Kage's door.

What kind of temptation is this? God, please HELP…

"Wow, look at you in your doctor suit. Hey Kage hey. How you doing?" Ember flirts.

"Mrs. Stoneshire, please have a seat."

Ember sits on his table.

"There's a chair. Please sit on it."

She strokes his chest. He grabs her hand. "Don't you **DARE** touch me. Have a seat or leave my office."

"Is this how you speak to your patients?" Ember snaps.

"You are **NOT** my patient. How may I help you Mrs. Stoneshire?"

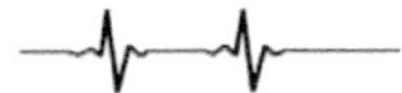

After the brief conversation with Ember, Kage ran to the bathroom and splashed water on his face. He immediately dials Vermont's number.

"She's back," Kage talks into the receiver.

"Calm down. Who are you talking about?"

"Ember."

"Your ex?"

Kage nods as though Vermont could see him.

"Kage? You there?"

"Sorry man, yes, Ember. The same one who ruined my life. The same one who can't seem to stop popping up from time to time. What is the meaning of this? Why am I being tested like this?"

"That's a question to ask Jesus."

"It's not supposed to be like this."

"What did you expect?" Vermont asks.

"I don't know. Just not Ember. That woman is a thorn in my flesh."

"We'll pray and ask God to reveal what HE wants you to gain from this experience. Do you have any feelings whatsoever towards Ember?"

"No, I can honestly say that. I never attached myself emotionally to any woman except Marwa and Brynn. Those were the only two."

"Well, it seems like Ember represents your **past** and you need to spend the next two weeks praying and fasting seriously against any remnants from your past. Because you've had many partners, you're bound to bump into them at some point or the other. Those spiritual ties need to be broken. You need to ensure that you've forgiven yourself, and allow the Holy Spirit to do HIS job of keeping you. The enemy **will** send women to distract you, but God is able to keep you from falling into temptation. I've seen you grow in this department. Since we met you haven't so much as gone on a date, although we've tried to connect you with some lovely women. You made it clear that you'd know your wife when you saw her. If that woman is Nouvel, then that's who we'll pray for."

"Thanks man."

"Any time," Vermont responds.

48

The doorbell rang. Kage hadn't expected anyone. He stares at his phone for missed calls.

Nothing.

To his dismay, Ember stood on his doorsteps.

"Can I come in?" she asks.

"Ember you should not be here. I don't want whatever drama you're bringing. I haven't seen you in years and we're not friends."

"Is that how Christians speak to people?"

"How may I help you?" Kage replies, annoyed.

"I came to find out information about my husband. The nurse said that you were off today."

"So, you show up at my house?"

Ember exhales in exasperation. "I made a mistake."

"By coming here? Yes, you did."

"No, by marrying Fox. You've always been the one that I wanted."

"This conversation isn't going anywhere. The fact is Ember, you are a **married woman**. There's no time for reflection of what *could've been*. I respect the sanctity of marriage. And also, I never loved you. What we had is over. I'm in a relationship and I'm not going to allow you or anyone from my past to mess that up."

"Who's this **lucky woman** that has caught the heart of the PLAYER of all PLAYERS?"

"That's none of your business," Kage retorts.

"Come on Kage, oblige me."

"Nouvel de Amico."

Ember's eyes widen. Suddenly she bursts into laughter. "My ex-best friend and my ex-boyfriend hooked up? How nasty. She got my sloppy seconds. I knew she was jealous of me, but—"

"Enough!" he snaps. "I will not have you disrespect Nouvel in any manner. And our relationship is none of your business."

"Y'all getting married?"

Kage stands in silence.

"Fine," Ember barks. "I will make sure to pay your little girlfriend a visit. I'm sure she doesn't know about our **many** encounters in and out of bed."

"Why are you doing this? Finding pleasure in trying to ruin someone's future?"

"Oh, that's rich coming from the likes of you MR. HUNTER. It doesn't matter how innocent you're acting now, EVERY SINGLE WOMAN in this country knows your name for all the wrong reasons. It's only a matter of time until Pseudo Saint Nouvel dumps you."

"Are you done?" he counters.

"Did she tell you that she was a harlot before, during, and after university? Do you know that about her?"

"Ember, I'm done talking to you. Please go tend to your husband. Leave me and mine alone." He walks back into the house, closing the door on her.

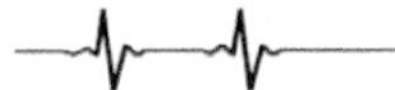

Kage kneels by his bedside to pray. He now understood what Xerses meant about making sure his lineage was clean.

> *Dear God, I come to You in the name of Jesus, asking that You help me deal with the past. I know Father that You have forgiven me, but after all these years I still don't feel good enough to be used by you. So many women can call my name as a man they've had sex with. I've ruined their lives because of my addiction.*

> *The number of women in my conquest book is in the triple digits. I don't know why You love me...*

Tears fill his eyes, as the magnitude of his past overwhelmed him.

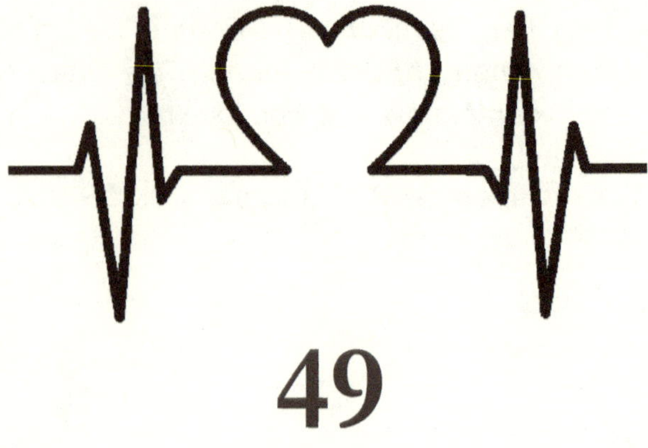

49

Vermont knocked on Kage's door.

"It's open," Kage cries out.

Watching his friend on the floor in agony, affected Vermont. Kage was like a brother to him. "Talk to me, man," Vermont requests.

"I don't know if I can do this. All those women. Ember is just one of hundreds. I can't even walk down the street without a side eye. My name is tarnished in Starr Islands because of my choice. How could God love me knowing that I've messed up so many lives? How many women are probably in therapy because of me?" Kage weeps.

"Kage, I understand what you're going through, but you can't erase your past. Get your Bible, let's read a passage."

Moments later, Kage brings his Bible.

"Turn to 1 Timothy 1:9-17. You read," Vermont instructs.

"Knowing this, that the law is not made for a righteous man, but for the lawless and disobedient, for the ungodly and for sinners, for unholy and profane, for murderers of fathers and murderers of mothers, for manslayers, for whoremongers, for them that defile themselves with mankind, for menstealers, for liars, for perjured persons, and if there be any other thing that is contrary to sound doctrine; According to the glorious gospel of the blessed God, which was committed to my trust.

And I thank Christ Jesus our Lord, who hath enabled me, for that he counted me faithful, putting me into the ministry; who was before a blasphemer, and a persecutor, and injurious: but I obtained mercy, because I did it ignorantly in unbelief. And the grace of our Lord was exceeding abundant with faith and love which is in Christ Jesus. This is a faithful saying, and worthy of all acceptation, that Christ Jesus came into the world to save sinners; of whom I am chief. Howbeit for this cause I obtained mercy, that in me first Jesus Christ might shew forth all longsuffering, for a pattern to them which should hereafter believe on him to life everlasting. Now unto the King eternal, immortal, invisible, the only wise God, be honour and glory for ever and ever. Amen," Kage read aloud.

"Amen. Stand up," Vermont says.

Kage does as instructed.

"What is your name?"

"Kage Hunter."

"Who are you?"

"I don't understand," Kage answers.

"Don't think. Just answer. Who are you?"

"Kage Hunter?"

"No, you are **forgiven** by the God of the universe. The King of Kings and Lord of Lords. In that passage of scripture Paul was explaining to Timothy about Christ' purpose on the earth. Jesus Christ came to save sinners. Paul said **I AM CHIEF OF SINNERS**. Meaning that Paul wasn't referring to his past, but present. His present status. Without Jesus Christ, Paul is a nobody. Without Jesus Christ, Paul is a sinner. A murderer. You're NOT the first hated man on the planet, Kage. Paul was. You think you have a body count because of sleeping with hundreds of women? The most talked about Apostle during our time was HATED during his. Are you getting it? Paul knew who he was before Christ, but he didn't allow that to affect his ministry. He used it as fuel for ministry. I AM CHIEF OF SINNERS, but I AM FORGIVEN. That's what Paul preached throughout the Gospels. His past didn't count him out of the race of God's CHOSEN ministers. God handpicked Paul **REGARDLESS** of past.

God used Paul to save the lives of millions, **REGARDLESS** of his past. People talked, mocked, rebuked, and laughed at Paul. They reminded him of his past, but his focus was his **FUTURE with God.** His desire was to be with God. Paul could've sulked about his past and why he wasn't good enough to complete the task that God called him for, but he didn't. Until his dying breath, Paul preached the Gospel of Jesus Christ."

The tears continued to flow down Kage's face.

"God loves you, Kage. Your past isn't a deterrent to your purpose. Once as you avail yourself and continuously stay on the Potter's wheel, there's no telling where HE'll take you. Trust HIM. Trust the process. The past is the past, it may rear its head from time to time, but don't give it authority over your future. That belongs to God. God is in control. Let HIM do HIS job. Let's pray…"

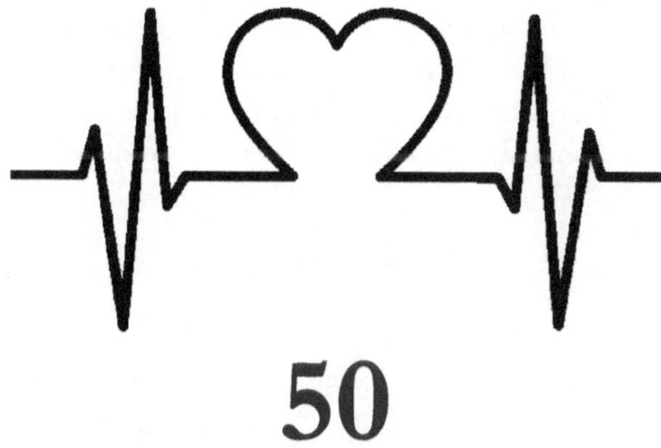

50

Thirty days after Kage spoke to Nouvel, God asked him to push for another sixty. It had been 90 days since he saw or spoke to Nouvel. As per initial instructions, he wasn't allowed to inquire about her. They never crossed paths in their daily routines. The extension served a greater purpose than being with Nouvel.

Kage had to forgive himself and allow God to lead. He spent so many years trying to save face or defend himself, but as Vermont pointed out, the decisions that he made was prior to conversion. He was a sinner during those years. No longer could he view himself as the old Kage, but daily put on the *new man. Renew his mind*, to reflect that of Christ.

Now that the time was up, he got ready to meet Nouvel for a serious conversation. Although he was nervous, he felt peace in his heart that things would be as God ordained.

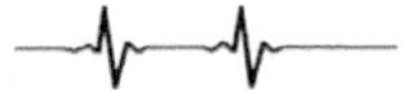

Nouvel hadn't expected to see her former friend, while shopping. Although she was an actress, her life was drama free. And the look on Ember's face oozed **incoming drama.**

"Hello, Nouvel," Ember greets in disdain.

"Hey Ember, how are you?"

"I heard about you and Kage. My ex. You have my sloppy seconds. First Rayce, now Kage. Can't you get a man of your own?"

"You never had Rayce."

"Oh, so you're defending your ex who dumped you because you were a slut?"

"Watch your mouth," Nouvel replies.

"Come off it. Don't act like you were an angel. We may have called you **saint**, but then we found out the truth. Just how many men did you sleep with?"

"Is there something I can help you with? We haven't spoken in years and here you are bringing up my past that I've already been forgiven for."

Ember laughs. "You and your religious delusions. ***Forgiven by god*,**" she mocks. "How pathetic. That actually makes you sleep well at night, KNOWING that you're just as **nasty** as that wannabee future fiancé of yours… KAGE HUNTER! Did you forget that he slept with almost every woman on and off campus?"

"Are you done? You're not doing anything to me by bringing up my past. I'm not that woman anymore."

"He was mine first," Ember snaps.

"Aren't you married? Why are you so worried about Kage?"

"He was mine first," she repeats.

"But, he's my last and forever. There's no contest here. Your pathetic attempt at seducing him. He's not that guy anymore."

"He'll always be ***that guy***."

"That's where you're wrong. God changes people."

"Uggh! Please. Stop with this religious talk. Fine! Have him. You'll always be a harlot…"

"I have no further words for you. You're the PAST, Ember. Please stay there. Have a good night!"

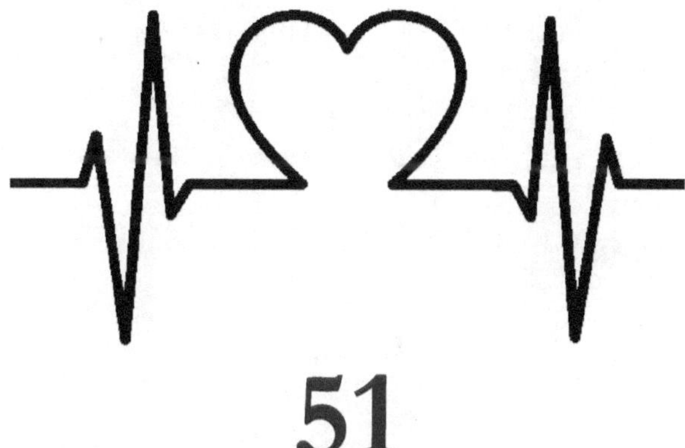

51

Solo Mio

Later that night, Kage waited for Nouvel in the restaurant. He paced the lobby as thoughts flooded his mind.

"Hi Kage," Nouvel says, greeting him with a hug.

"You look beautiful."

"Thanks," she smiles.

"Our table is this way." He leads her to a table in the center of the restaurant.

"There's no one else here."

"I rented it out. This is a private conversation."

"I'm really nervous," she reveals.

Kage nods. "Me too."

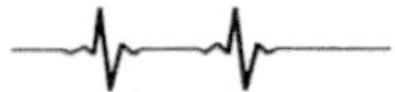

"Do you want to go first or should I?" Kage asks, when they sat down.

"I'll go first," Nouvel chuckles. "This has been an extremely difficult 90 days for me. When Belle-Amore told me that there's an extension I must admit I was not happy. I thought that God was dangling you in front of me at the conference and then took you away. I realized that the time apart was not about us at all. God had to deal with some things in me. Unforgiveness was one of them. Although I know that nothing has happened between you and Ember since, she has been the most constant person from your past in my mind. Only a few hours ago we had a confrontation, she called me names and laughed at our relationship—"

"You saw her?" he interrupts.

"Let me finish."

"Sorry."

"I understand that we both had ugly pasts. Neither of us are saints. But, as Christians none of us are perfect and we all have a story. People like to highlight sins based on levels of intensity when in God's eyes they're all sins. Jesus Christ died for **all sins**. HE **forgives all sins**. So how dare we try to say who gets saved and who doesn't. Thank God there's only one God. If we as humans had to pick people for salvation, no one would be saved. After day 30, I went into a time of prayer and fasting. God highlighted some things in my life that HE wanted me to do and you were there alongside me. That's all I have to say. You can go now," she smiles nervously.

Kage motioned for her to stand up.

"What is this about?"

He got down on his knees. "I had no speech planned; God already gave me the peace that you were my wife. HE instructed me to wait for the word, *alongside*. That's all the confirmation I needed." Without waiting a minute longer, Kage pulled out an engagement ring box and held it up to Nouvel…

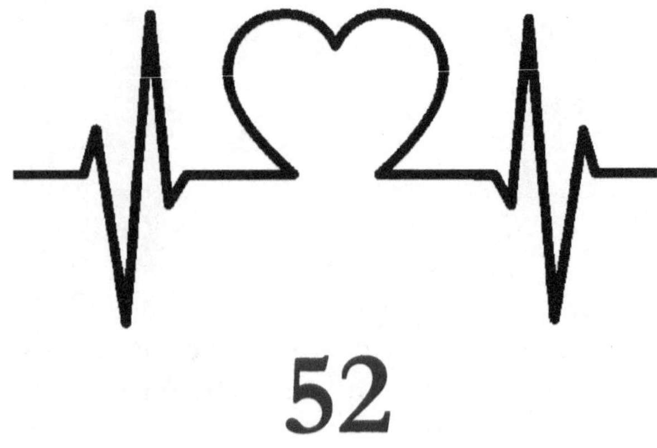

52

September
Holbrook Grand Hotel

Kage looks out the hotel window. "I told you I'd marry her one day…"

Xerses laughs, "I'm happy that my sister found a man who loves her in spite of her past. Sorry I misjudged you."

"That's alright. I never knew that my annoying roommate would one day become my brother-in-law."

"Don't get all mushy on me."

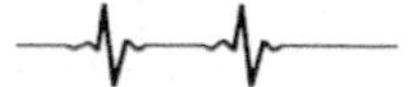

Bridal Suite

Nouvel looked around the room at all the women who helped her. It was true what the saying said… *healed women speak differently.*

"Congratulations girlie, I'm so proud of and happy for you. I can tell that Kage loves you," Tahira greets.

"Turn around, turn around," Kaiora chuckles. "You're a vision in white. Wait until Mr. Hunter sees you."

"You think he'll like it?" Nouvel asks.

"YES!" Kaiora answers.

"Knock! Knock!" Mr. de Amico announces, entering the room. "Is my beauty ready?"

"Yes, dad," Nouvel replies, with tears streaming down her face.

"We'll meet you downstairs," Tahira says.

Kaiora walks out of the room behind her.

"This is happening. My beauty is finally getting married. I am thankful that God blessed you with a man who loves you. Your brother speaks highly of Kage."

"Yes, they go wayyyy back," she chuckles.

"Well then, let's get you to that altar."

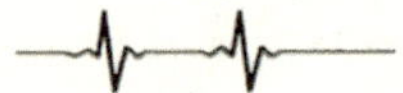

"Wow, double royalty in my room," Kage claps. "Mr. Tavario Mikos, King of Acting himself, *Vias* Royalty, and Mr. Amerigio Canzoniere, Pastor and Mentor of the Crown Prince of Lucca, Kalevi Náousa. Thank you so much for being a part of this day. It means a lot to my wife and I."

The men laugh.

"I do hope you and your lovely wife will join Kaiora and I in Italy for vacation someday," Amerigio verbalizes.

"No doubt about it. Nouvel loves Italy," Kage replies.

"They all do," Tavario chimes. "Alright, I think it's about that time."

Kage looks at the wall clock.

Time to get married to most beautiful woman that ever graced this earth…

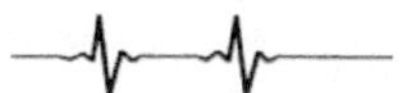

Kage watched as Nouvel walked down the aisle. Tears flowed as he reflected on their very first meeting, the nerves he felt at 18 trying to *step to her.* He remembered her no nonsense attitude. Even back then he knew that women like Nouvel were rare. Laughter escaped his mouth as he thought about it… This woman didn't give him the time of day and yet, she was going to be his wife. God really turned around both of their lives for the better.

KAGE HUNTER had a new title: HUSBAND!

It had a nice ring to it. And he would be sure to take his role seriously.

"There she is," Xerses announces, as Nouvel made her way closer to the altar. "Your bride."

Kage' face turned crimson…

Look at her.

My wife.

Perfect.

Simply perfect.

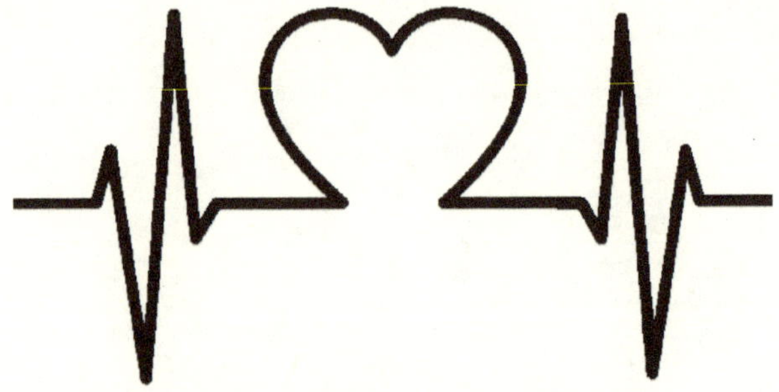

From The Author

Life isn't perfect and we all have a past. But that doesn't exclude us from the *"plans that God has for us"*. No matter who we are, what we did, how **UGLY** our story is, God can turn it into a beautiful testimony. Don't let your history hinder you from all that God has in store for you.

Comparison is a killer.

Sin is sin.

People will talk, laugh, and tease…

You won't feel like you *"deserve anything good"* because of what you've done.

But throughout history, we see that God doesn't give us what we "deserve". Allow HIS love and mercy to wash over you. No one will **EVER** love you like the Father (the Definition of Unconditional Agape Love).

You are loved by the Father (God) and no one can take that away from you. Accept His love today and watch how HE will turn your story around…

~Theastarr Valerie

www.ingramcontent.com/pod-product-compliance
Lightning Source LLC
LaVergne TN
LVHW090558110826
845146LV00001B/170